AWAKENING

CLAUDIA CANGILLA MCADAM

AWAKENING

A CROSSROADS IN TIME BOOK

SOPHIA INSTITUTE PRESS

THE PUBLISHING DIVISION OF

THOMAS MORE COLLEGE of LIBERAL ARTS   HOLY SPIRIT COLLEGE

Sophia Institute Press®
Box 5284, Manchester, NH 03108
1-800-888-9344
www.SophiaInstitute.com

Printed in the United States of America

Library of Congress Cataloging-in-Publication Data

McAdam, Claudia Cangilla.
    Awakening : a novel / by Claudia Cangilla McAdam.
        p. cm.
    "A crossroads in time book."
    Summary: Eighth-grader Ronni's Catholic faith has been sorely tested in the year since her father and brother were killed, but during a critical illness she is transported to Jerusalem at the end of Christ's life and gains insight into His sacrifice and what it means for her.
        ISBN 978-1-933184-61-6 (pbk. : alk. paper) [1. Faith — Fiction. 2. Space and time — Fiction. 3. Jesus Christ — Fiction. 4. Jerusalem — History — 1st century — Fiction. 5. Bible. N.T. — History of Biblical events — Fiction. 6. Death — Fiction. 7. Catholics — Fiction.] I. Title.
    PZ7.M47819Aw 2009
    [Fic] — dc22
                                                                                    2009032978

www.claudiamcadam.com

In honor of my parents, Louis and Patricia Cangilla,
who gave me life, who showered me with love,
and who raised me in the faith,
living out Deuteronomy 6:6-7.

AWAKENING

CHAPTER ONE

"I hate you!" I slammed the door into the jamb with a boom, and it shivered the walls down the hall and into the living room and dining room. The china in the cabinet tinkled against glass shelves. The grandfather clock in the entry groaned a gong, even though it was still ten minutes before the hour.

In my bedroom, the knickknacks on the bookshelf tottered and rattled. Out of the corner of my eye, I saw the trophy on the top shelf wobble and teeter side to side, like a drunk staggering along a line. I stretched out my arm, but too late. It somersaulted to the floor. The golden, pony-tailed soccer girl, her leg outstretched with ball balanced against her arch, landed upside-down on the floor. Her head and foot snapped off, and the rest of her body broke free from the trophy's pedestal.

"Ouch!" I said, rubbing the back of my head, as if the injury had been to me and not to the figurine that was supposed to represent me.

I picked up the pieces. The "MVP" plaque had popped off the fake-marble base. "Most Vocal Person," I said, changing the real meaning of the abbreviation. "Why can't I just keep my big mouth shut?" I dumped the mess onto my desk.

I raked my fingers through my hair — long, like the soccer girl's, but not straight and golden like hers. Mine was as dark as night, and it bumped its way down my back in waves that could turn into ringlets if the humidity was high enough.

My belt loops scraped against the door as I slid down and sat on the floor. A human doorstop. I half expected my mother to storm into my room for another showdown. She wouldn't get in here now even if she *did* try to bust in . . . or come softly knocking in a few minutes, calling my name.

It hadn't gone at all like I thought it would. I was so happy when I walked through the front door. It's not every day that someone like Tabby Long invites you to go with her family to their mountain cabin. Cabin, nothing. It's a two-story, four-bedroom, three-bath palace with a hot tub on the deck and two snowmobiles perched on a trailer in the three-car garage.

"Tonight? They're going up tonight?" Mom asked. She slid her chair back slightly from the kitchen table and turned her book over to hold her place.

Although it was upside-down, I could pick out one of the words in the title: *Exodus*. That seemed right. It was an exodus from this house that I had planned.

"Actually, before dinner," I said. "Since we don't have school on Holy Thursday or Good Friday, Mr. Long wants to leave early to beat the Easter crowd. This is the last weekend the slopes will be open. And if we get up there by dinner, he can night-ski under the lights."

Mom glanced up at me. She knew all about Mr. Long's eye disease. Some scary-sounding thing called uveitis. The white part of his eyes looked horribly bloodshot most of the time, and a ring of cloudiness circled the irises. Tabby said that he could go blind.

"He can't ski during the day anymore," I said. "The sunlight reflecting off the snow hurts his eyes. This might be the last time he can see well enough to ski at all."

She nodded her head. "I know." She looked squarely at me. "They don't think his eyes are going to get better."

If that was true, then surely she'd let me go. "Tabby says that sometimes the pain is so bad, he can't go to work. Please, Mom? I don't know when they might be going to the cabin again — if ever."

"But you've only been back to school since Monday."

"I feel fine." I swallowed hard without flinching, as proof that the strep throat that had kept me home for a whole week was completely gone. So what if it still hurt a tiny bit? She didn't need to know that.

"It's not that," Mom said. "Your school work. You've got a lot to make up." Her raised eyebrow challenged me to deny it.

"I'm a fast reader, and I get good grades." Well, usually. "I'll bring it with me. I'll work on it every day." Yeah, right.

Mom stood up and paused for a moment, her eyes on the table. I could tell she was considering it. "And when would you be back?" Her head cocked toward me.

I silently drew in a big breath. This was it. "Sunday morning. I'd be back in time for the last Easter Mass, I'm sure," I quickly added.

Mom nodded, still thinking, and kneaded her forehead with her fingertips. She knew how important this was for me. Tabby might have been the new girl at school last September, but now there was no one in the whole eighth grade more popular. Some of the other girls had spent weekends at her cabin this winter. And now, with just two months left of school, she had finally asked me.

Mom slipped back into her chair and placed her palms on the table. "Ronni, this is the Easter Triduum. Why would you want to be gone during the holiest time of year?" She spread her fingers and raised them slightly to punctuate her question.

She wanted to know *why*? Wasn't she *ever* my age? Didn't she remember what it was like to have fun?

"But I'll be back in time for Easter Mass." Even if I didn't want to be. "Mr. Long will be sure to get me back whenever you say." That's it, suck up. "He's always on time. I think he got that from being in the army for so long."

"And the Mass of the Last Supper tomorrow? Did you forget you were supposed to serve?" I had. Why did I sign up to do that? Being an altar server when I started two years ago in sixth grade was cool. But now . . . I was going to quit at the end of the school year. I was still serving only because Mom wanted me to.

"And you'd miss Stations of the Cross on Good Friday," she said. "What will you be doing instead?"

Just about anything else, I wanted to say. "I don't know . . . we —"

"He died for *you*, you know."

Here we go again, I thought. "Well, I didn't ask him to!"

Mom opened her mouth, but I didn't let her get a word out.

"Dad would have let me go." That was a low blow, for two reasons. One, because Dad wasn't a Catholic. And two, because it hadn't even been a year since Dad and Steven had died. I started to say something else, then promptly shut my trap. Talking about Dad and Steven was like picking at a scab. I didn't feel like adding a scar today.

Mom shut her eyes and pinched her lips together in a thin line. She thought she could dam up the pain that way. She was pretty good at it. She opened her eyes and looked at me straight on, but she didn't rise to the bait. She didn't say anything about what Dad would have done. We both knew that that didn't matter. Not now.

"So you don't understand why the Lord suffered and died for you? For us?"

"No," I said honestly.

Why would anybody die for somebody they didn't know? I mean, I got the whole bit about salvation. Forgiveness of sin, getting to heaven. It was the sacrifice part that didn't make sense to me. Couldn't that have happened any other way? I guess I had a bit of Doubting Thomas in me. I believed in Jesus, I really did. I just never understood why he had to *die*. I always wondered why no one really tried to stop it. I would have. His death seemed so unfair. I just didn't get it. Nothing was worth dying for.

"And you think you're going to learn why our Savior died for you while you're at Tabby's? I don't think so. Pay attention during the next few days, and maybe you'll get it."

She stood up, the chair legs scraping harshly against the wooden floor, and she huffed into the living room. I knew exactly what she was doing. She'd settle into the rocker, and either pick up her knitting or grab her rosary from the end table, praying to the Blessed Mother to give her strength. Or to ask her Son to do something to save my soul.

One time she had entwined her first two fingers together and held them up to me. "Mary and I are like this," she had said. She had grown up without a mom, so I could understand her turning to Jesus' mother for comfort and help. I knew what it was like to have a parent leave you, dying for no good reason.

I had to give it one more chance, but I couldn't think of a convincing argument. I followed her into the living room. "Please?"

No answer. I stamped my foot. "You never let me do anything!" A lie, and still no answer. "You are so mean!" And with that, I stomped off to my room.

As I sat on my bedroom floor, tears pooled behind my lower eyelids; mini waterfalls tumbled down my cheeks. My throat felt as if I were wearing a too-tight turtleneck. The glands under my jawbone seemed swollen and achy. The backs of my hands itched. My eczema became irritated when my nerves got out of whack. I scratched at the scaly patches until they almost bled. Ugly hands. I hated them.

"Ronni!"

At first, I wasn't sure I heard my name being called, but a tapping on my bedroom window confirmed that I wasn't hallucinating.

"Ronni!"

Ohmigosh! I'd forgotten I'd left Tabby standing on the front porch while I went inside to talk to Mom. I hauled myself off the floor and leaned over my desk to slide the window open.

She stood on the other side, the sun highlighting the paler streaks in her blonde hair. With no screen between us, she propped her elbows on the windowsill and rested her chin in her palms. "I guess you're not coming."

"You heard?"

The dimples in her cheeks showed themselves. "It was hard not to. It sounded like a bomb went off in there."

I plopped into the desk chair. "Sorry."

"Why don't you come anyway?" Her eyelids closed slightly as she leaned in a bit. "Just grab your stuff and climb out the window," she whispered. "Look what I brought."

She dug into the pocket of her fleece jacket. Blue, of course. Tabby always wore blue because she said it brought out the color of her eyes. Only her clothes weren't just "blue," to hear Tabby describe them. Her pajamas were "robin's egg," her swimsuit "azure," her favorite blouse "aquamarine," and her velvet skirt "cobalt." Lucky for her our school uniforms were blue. Or should I say "navy"? I don't know what she would have done if she'd had to wear Sacred Heart School's fire-engine red.

"Here," she said, pulling from her pocket a DVD in a clear plastic case: *The Wizard of Oz.* "We can watch it together at the cabin." For our big assignment in religion class, we had to pick a classic movie from Mr. Josephson's list and analyze the religious themes in it. A month ago I'd picked my all-time favorite oldie-but-goodie, and Tabby picked the same one.

Mr. Josephson had given us permission to team up and work on our paper together. That's how we started to be friends.

"Just come," she said again.

For a moment I was tempted. We'd probably be up at the cabin before Mom even called me to set the table for dinner.

"I can't. I'm supposed to serve at Mass tomorrow and . . ."

Tabby grunted. Loudly. "Doesn't all this church-goin' ever get to you?" She folded her arms across the sill and stared at me. Tabby's family wasn't Catholic. They weren't anything, as far as I could tell. She said her folks sent her to St. Augustine's for the discipline and the academics. It sure wasn't to learn the faith, even though she was required to take Mr. Josephson's religion classes.

I glued my eyes to the desk and rolled a pencil back and forth under my palm. When I realized my scaly hands were exposed to Tabby's full view, I quickly slipped them behind my back and deliberately didn't look at her. My teachers and my friends might have known about my eczema. That didn't mean they liked looking at it. I certainly didn't.

I never let people see my hands, if I could help it. The eczema along my cuticles caused my nails to thicken and grow out yellowed and bumpy. I'd tuck my hands between my knees when I sat, or cross my arms and fold my hands under my biceps. I loved winter when I could pull long sleeves down as far as they'd go — to my fingertips, if I was lucky.

"I'm sorry," I finally said, my eyes still on my desk. "I really want to go to the cabin. Maybe you could ask me again some other time —"

"Hi, Mark!" Tabby's voice came from far away. I looked up. She had left the window and was walking past the neighbor's open garage where Mark was working on his car. She wouldn't ask me again. There wouldn't be another time for me.

CHAPTER TWO

Mark pulled his head of dark curls out from under the hood of a Mustang that was as old as my mom. "Hey, Tab," he called back to her, his face spreading into a big grin. I ducked off to the side of the window in case he looked my way. Yeah, right. I wished.

Mark had been my big brother Steven's best friend. They'd been in the same classes and on the same baseball team forever. They'd even picked the same Confirmation name — John. Mark was supposed to be in the car with Dad and Steven that night last summer. It was the guys' final game of the season before they started high school, and Mark had planned to ride home with Dad and Steven, but his folks showed up during the last inning. Lucky for Mark.

"I'm so sorry, Ronni," Mark had said after the cops left that awful night. He let me sob against his shoulder, and he cried, too. Then he prayed with me. I never would have thought to do that. How could God have let this happen to Dad and Steven?

Mark had always been like another big brother to me, but since that night, I felt differently about him. Closer. I didn't care that my mom said she wouldn't be surprised if he became a priest one day. I began making other plans for him. Plans I could never act on, though. Whenever he was near, I started sweating buckets, and it seemed like I was always saying something stupid or staring at him when he wasn't looking.

At the sound of more voices, I remembered where I was and peeked out the window. Mr. Simon from across the street stood in Mark's garage with his hands on his hips, examining the engine of the old Mustang. Mr. Simon had worked in an auto-repair shop before he moved his family here from Jamaica, and whenever he had time after work, he'd come over and help with the car. With months to go before Mark got his license, they were sure to get that thing up and running in time for him to drive it. And to take me to homecoming in the fall. Well, a girl could dream, couldn't she?

The little Simon boys, Alex and R.J., kicked a soccer ball from Mark's yard to mine. I babysat them every Saturday when their folks went out on their "date night." Funny, but I was always available.

"Hi, Ronni," the boys yelled. Uh-oh. Busted. "Come play soccer with us!" Their favorite activity when I watched them.

Mr. Simon glanced up, and Mark looked my way and waved. "Hey, peanut!" he called.

Peanut. Not the first time I had heard that. Although I was the fastest runner on my soccer team, I was also the smallest, and the opposing players often used to taunt me about my size. That is, until I dribbled past them and drove the ball into the net. When others called me "shrimp" or "shorty," they did it in meanness, but Mark's nickname for me was always said with a smile.

My face flushed, and I quickly waved back and stepped away from the window, hoping they couldn't see my blush from that distance.

With my window directly across from Mark's garage, I had a great view of him whenever he was out working on the car, which made it hard to get homework done sometimes. But the last month I'd kept the curtain closed most of the time, ever since the evening I'd taken a bath and walked into my fully lit room wrapped in a towel. I'd forgotten I'd left the shade up. The towel slipped off right as I walked past the window. I could hear music coming from the Mustang and knew Mark was working on it. I hit the floor immediately. Had he seen me? Was I going to ruin him for the priesthood? Probably just the opposite, I figured. After getting an eyeful of me, he'd go straight to the minor seminary instead of entering his sophomore year of high school in September.

I couldn't be sure what he'd glimpsed, if anything, but he had avoided my eyes every time I'd seen him after that, which could have meant nothing — or everything. It didn't matter because, since then, I'd been too embarrassed to talk to him.

I took one more peek out the window, but he was gone. What did catch my eye, though, was the "For Sale" sign in our front yard. A lump formed in my throat. Dad's life insurance wouldn't be enough to let us hang on to the house for too much longer. The savings account got tapped out when he opened his own law firm. That included our college funds, which he was sure he would be able to replenish in no time. So much for my dreams of med school.

My eyes burned, and through the gathering tears, I examined the pieces of the fractured trophy on my desk. I couldn't mend the broken chunks of the plastic girl. And I'd never get the chance to try to heal humans either, I realized. I swept the pile into the trash can.

I stepped up to my full-length mirror and examined my eyes more intently. Red-rimmed lids circled the bloodshot whites. I wondered if Mr. Long's eye disease was contagious. Whenever I blinked, my head pounded. That's what I got for crying. What I needed was a shower.

I noiselessly swung open my door and tiptoed down the hall to the bathroom. As I closed the bathroom door, I heard the doorbell ring. For a minute I thought it might be Tabby. But when Mom didn't call to me, I knew that Tabby was gone. Despondently, I started the shower, peeled off my school uniform pants and oxford shirt, and left the clothes piled on the floor with my socks and underwear. The hot water felt wonderful, but just the effort of washing my hair tired out my arms. What was wrong with me? I shut off the water and reached for a towel. Nothing. I slid the shower curtain open, my skin goose-pimpling as the cooler air outside the shower hit me. Where were the towels? The racks were bare.

Of course. This was Wednesday. Mom cleaned the bathroom and washed the towels on Wednesdays. Why hadn't she hung up fresh ones? The linen closet was out in the hall. I'd drip all the way there. And it would be just my luck that Mark would be standing in the living room talking to my mom and looking straight down the hall at me.

I decided to dry off with my clothes, but stupid me had left the corner of the shower curtain outside the tub, and my uniform was sopping wet.

I wrung out my hair and stood on the cold tile floor, a trickle of water snaking down my back. Mom had even taken the bath mat. In the cabinet under the sink, there was nothing to use to dry off. I searched the drawers, and in the bottom one, I pulled out a big white rectangle. It was a thin cotton towel that we used for drying dishes or to put over delicate fabrics when Mom ironed. She called it a "tea towel." It would have to do.

I wrapped the cloth around my hair and tucked in the ends. By then, my body was almost dry, but I didn't want to streak down the hall naked to my room. Mom's old nightgown was shoved in the back of the drawer. She wore it as a smock when she colored her hair. I snagged it and slipped it over my head. The plain, beige cotton fabric was worn, but soft and cozy. It reached nearly to my ankles and had long sleeves, which I cuffed, and a simple V-neck opening.

The door creaked slightly as I pulled it open. I paused to listen. The television was on in the family room. No, wait, it wasn't the TV. Mom was talking with someone. Maggie. Yuck! That freak with her skimpy clothes and multiple piercings was always sniffing around Mark — like she used to do with Steven. It didn't matter that he was a year younger than she was — he was still a guy, and when it came to Maggie, any and *every* guy would do.

It was just my luck that when Mom started mentoring at the high school, Maggie got assigned to her. Somehow Mom had convinced Maggie to come to youth group at church a few times. She probably went for the same reason I did: Mark. Her appearance there always caused quite a stir, especially with the guys. But the last time I saw her, there wasn't an inch of midriff showing on Maggie. A long-sleeved shirt covered the "Bad Girl" tattoo on her bicep, and the number of earrings in each ear was down to two. But the eyelids were still smoky and the lips really red.

Mom must have quoted First Corinthians to her as she always did to me, echoing St. Paul's words that our bodies were temples of the Holy Spirit. How did I get so lucky that I had not only a retired college Scripture professor for a religion teacher, but also a mother who scolded me with Bible verses? Mom was always throwing St. Paul's words at me and then cautioning me to not wear skimpy tank tops, short shorts, or low-rise jeans. So what if Maggie *had* been listening to her? I still didn't like that girl.

I sneaked back to my room, sat down at the desk, and fished a handful of sunflower seeds out of a bag in the drawer. I scattered them on the outside window ledge and slid the glass closed. It wasn't long before a cream-colored pigeon swooped to a landing and began pecking at the seeds. I'd been feeding him for weeks, and we were slowly becoming friends. I was betting that soon I'd be able to reach out, and he'd let me hold him in my hand.

While he cracked open seed after seed, I propped my feet on my desk and went to work taking the polish off my toenails. That old purple shade just wasn't going to work with the new shoes I planned to wear to Easter Mass — red leather slides with two-inch stacked wooden heels that made me look a little taller and feel much older.

I moved from left to right, rubbing a cotton ball soaked in polish-remover across the nails, beginning with my pinky toe on my left foot. By the time I reached my other little toe, the cotton ball was dry and the bottle of polish-remover empty. I didn't care. I could have picked off the remaining polish, but the throbbing in my temples made me lose all interest. That nail was tiny, and nobody would see the fleck of purple on it when it was tucked behind the strap of the red shoes.

I folded my arms on my desk and rested my head on them so I could look at the picture of Dad and Steven in a frame just inches from my face. Thoughts of them filled my mind, and as always happened when I remembered the night of the accident, anger seeped in. I wasn't with them that night. If I had been, maybe I could have saved them. But I wasn't, and they died for nothing.

In my head I recreated what must have happened and played out the scene: on their way home from the baseball game, Dad and Steven pull over to help a guy who had crashed into the guard rail on the winding road leading up to our neighborhood. They get the old guy out of his car and start to push it out of the way when another car whips around the curve. The driver doesn't see them until it is too late. My dad and brother go flying.

I see the old guy off to the side of the road. Drunk. Not a scratch on him. No license. Not even in the country legally. No job. Borrowed car. A nobody.

I shook my head to make the images go away. I sat up and rubbed at the pain in my forehead. A nap. That's what I needed. I hadn't dried my hair, and I was still in Mom's old nightgown, but I didn't care. I slipped into bed and pulled the covers up under my chin. Then the shaking started. I was cold on the inside and burning on the outside. I could barely squeeze a drop of saliva down my throat, and my body hurt everywhere — right down to my eyelashes.

I wanted everything that I had no energy to get: water, Tylenol, socks, a hot-water bottle . . . and, I hated to admit it, my mom. My eyelids were so hard to open, they might as well have been garage doors. And when I finally cracked them a bit, the door to my bedroom seemed miles away. I tried to call for my mother, but the effort of attempting to push air through my vocal cords made my throat feel like the inside of a furnace.

Hot tears rolled from the outside corners of my eyes and down into my ears. I couldn't move, I couldn't talk, and I could barely breathe. One thought kept rolling through my mind: I was dying. I was dying.

CHAPTER THREE

It was like being in one of those dreams where you know you're dreaming, but you don't care. Quiet, calm, and peace bound me tightly. The sky looked hazy and out-of-focus, as if it were dusted with powdered sugar. Then the center rippled, and through a rift, a white dove emerged, wings flapping. It flew closer and closer, and I could feel soft waves of cool air wash over my face with each beat of a wing. It settled on my shoulder but continued to flutter its feathers, softly caressing my cheek.

While I could see all this, I couldn't physically open my eyes; they felt sewn shut. Weighted down by metal. Gradually, I realized that it wasn't a dove's wing grazing my face, but fingers. Several scents blended together. Fish. Herbs. Earth. Sweat. Man.

Slowly, my hearing engaged, and the sound of music reached my ears. Flutes playing somewhere outside. Mournful notes hovered around my head.

A murmur of voices floated to me, punctuated by my mother's sobbing, "Seraphina!" That was weird. Why was she using my middle name?

"She will be fine," a woman's voice said.

"You must have faith," added a man.

My brain felt clogged with cotton, but from its depths, I registered that they weren't speaking English. Yet I understood them completely.

The fingers ceased stroking my cheek, and a warm hand rested lightly along my jaw line.

"Talitha koum," a man said. "Little girl, I say to you, arise!"

Air filled my lungs, and my eyelids flew open. A bearded man sat perched on the edge of my bed, his hip touching my thigh, his left hand gripping mine, his right hand still resting against my face.

Suddenly, I was sitting upright. He hadn't lifted me, and I had made no effort to get in that position myself, but there I was, sitting up and feeling fine. Off to my left, I heard my mother stifle a gasp. Then her voice filled the room, loud and clear. "Bless the LORD, O my soul; and all that is within me, bless his holy name!"

The words seemed familiar to me. Weren't they the opening line of a psalm? In my religion class, Mr. Josephson made each of us memorize and recite a psalm for our midterm exam. Had one of my classmates picked this one? Is that why I knew it?

Apparently, I wasn't the only one who had heard it. After my mother prayed the first line, everyone else in the room picked up on the recitation. "Bless the LORD, O my soul, and forget not all his bene-fits, who forgives all your iniquity, who heals all your diseases," — my mother choked out a sob — "who redeems your life from the pit, who crowns you with steadfast love and mercy, who satisfies you with good as long as you live so that your youth is renewed like the eagle's."

My gaze never left the man sitting on my bed as I watched him, too, pray the psalm. His complexion was dark; his shoulder-length wavy hair was shiny black. My eyes were interlocked with his as if a tractor beam had me in its grip. How could it be that eyes so dark could have so much light and life in them? He was smiling at me with his whole face as well as his mouth, even though he was praying, and although I'd never seen him before, I was certain I had known him my whole life.

Behind him, the door was open, and the blaze of light spilling into the room illuminated the hair along the top curve of his head in a semicircle of brightness. Then a movement behind him caught my attention. Three men stood at the foot of the bed, their heads bowed, their lips moving in prayer. They reminded me of Hunk, Zeke, and Hickory, the farm hands huddled around Dorothy in her room at the end of *The Wizard of Oz*. But instead of overalls, they wore what looked like bathrobes.

"Hunk" and "Zeke" must have been brothers, they looked so much alike, but the older one was a couple of inches shorter and a bit scruffier than the other. Not a trace of stubble shadowed the chin of the younger one, still a teenager for sure, and not a bad-looking one at that. A barrel-chested "Hickory" looked up at me with serious eyes, a mane of dark, coarse hair flecked with gray framing his face and blending in with his wiry beard.

I closed my eyes and shook my head to clear it. To try to wake up. And when I opened my eyes again as the psalm ended, I saw silhouetted in the doorway a curly-haired figure whose face I didn't need to see to recognize: Mark.

The man sitting on my bed squeezed my hand, then let go. "Give her something to eat," he instructed.

At first I thought the woman who approached my bed was a nun. She wore a black robe, and a veil of charcoal gray framed a beautiful face. A kind face. An older, feminine version of the face of the man sitting on the edge of my bed.

Her hands cradled a wooden bowl filled with dried figs, which she offered to me. I picked one up and held it a moment, remembering my dad. During the holidays, his law firm used to send trays of dried fruit to their clients, and he always saw to it that one was delivered to our family as well. Mom liked the dates best. The apricot and pear halves were Steven's favorites, but I loved the sweet gritty insides of the figs. We didn't get a tray last Christmas.

I bit into the fruit, but my throat was so dry, I couldn't get the morsel down. "Milk," my mother said, and a cup found its way into my hands.

I swigged down a big gulp and immediately choked, the liquid backing up in my throat and fizzing into my nose. Ick! What kind of milk was this? It wasn't cold, it wasn't skim, and it wasn't from a cow. A bleating goat outside gave away the source.

Gentle laughter washed over me. The man on the edge of my bed, who must have been a doctor, patted my leg once and rose.

"Thank you, thank you," my mother said as she grasped his hands in hers and brought them to her lips.

She turned to the woman. "Miriam," she said, her voice cracking.

Miriam set down the fig bowl, hugged my mother, and smiling at me, followed the men out of the room. She pulled the door closed behind her, shutting off the opening in which Mark no longer stood.

"Seraphina!" My mother drew me to my feet and snaked her arms around me. "I thought you were . . ." She nearly squeezed the breath out of me, and underneath my cheek, I could feel her chest quivering.

I pulled back slightly and looked, really looked at my mom. Her face was the same, except for the gray circles under her tear-moistened eyes, but her clothing was plain, dark and old-fashioned. Really old-fashioned. A simple floor-length shift of rough, black fabric with a leather rope belt knotted at the side.

My eyes traveled up and down her clothes, then scanned the room. Everything was so strange. A feeling of panic rushed from my gut and escaped my lips in a small, strangled noise.

"Shhh," Mom whispered. "You are safe. At home. In our sleeping room."

I closed my eyes, rubbed them, opened them again, and looked at the room in detail. Sparsely furnished. Small. Dark. Another bed across from mine — my mother's? Dirt floor, stone walls. All in black and white like an old television show. Not my bedroom at all.

I couldn't get a grip on where I was. *When* I was. *Who* I was. I went to the closed door. The rough metal handle had a shiny spot where thumbs had worn it smooth. I pulled on the thick-planked wood, and it squeaked open on old hinges. The monotone interior of the room yielded to a colorful outdoors. I gasped.

I stood in the entrance, looking out onto a courtyard brilliant with the afternoon sun. My milk provider, recently shorn, I noted, was tethered to a stake, blissfully chewing her cud and twitching her long, floppy ears at pesky flies.

On the ground, a raised, circular layer of square-cut stones with an opening in the center looked as if it could be an in-ground hot tub, but weathered ropes coiled like cobras and scattered wooden buckets told me it was a well of some sort.

Other rooms of the house faced this courtyard. An open set of stairs stretched up to the flat rooftop. Colorful mats, rugs, and lengths of cloth draped the roof's low wall. Laundry day.

A palm tree grew in one corner of the courtyard. The first palm tree I'd ever seen in person. Slender green finger leaves waved at me in the gentle breeze. In the shade of the tree sat a stool surrounded by cloth sacks overflowing with raw wool, some of which I guessed came from the nearby goat. A long stick with a stone attached at the bottom rested against the stool. I had no idea what it was.

I looked over at the goat, which stopped her chewing, cocked her head, and returned my gaze. "Toto, I don't think we're in Kansas anymore." I stopped at the sound of my voice. The words had formed in my brain in English but tumbled from my mouth in Aramaic. My hand flew to my mouth. I could speak another language! Me, who was still *muy stinko* after taking Spanish for two years, could suddenly speak Aramaic.

CHAPTER FOUR

My mother touched my shoulder, and I turned to face her. "Mom, I'm so confused . . ."

"What is it?" she asked.

"Well, when I was —" When I was what? Sick? Asleep? Dead? By way of explanation, my eyes darted to the bed against the wall.

"Yes?" Mom led me to the edge of the bed where we sat down together on a mattress that rustled of straw. Not quite the down-filled mattress-topper I was used to.

Where should I begin?

"I was living in another place. Another time. You were still my mom. Dad and Steven were gone." I halted, suddenly hopeful. They weren't by any chance still alive, were they? Mom's face sank, and her head bowed. That answered that.

"Things were different. Our house. Our clothes. Everything."

She cupped my face in her hands. "A dream," she said. "Your fever was so high. You were saying strange things. I have no doubt your dreams were troubling ones. I was not sure you would live." Her voice caught in her throat. "I am not sure you did not die." She pressed her lips to my forehead, then sat back. "Maybe God blessed you with a vision. He blessed me by returning you to me."

"But it was real. So real. You and I had a fight," I said. She nodded, a soft smile curling up the corners of her mouth.

"We *did* fight, didn't we?" I asked.

"A disagreement. Not our first and probably not our last." She grinned.

"I'm so sorry," I said.

"I know. And I hope you understand why you must be here for the Seder meal and not off with Tabitha."

Seder? Didn't she mean Easter? "I know," I answered. But in reality, I didn't know anything.

Mark cleared his throat, delicately announcing his presence.

My mother rose from the bed and gestured to him. "Oh, Mark, come in," she said. I crossed my arms over my chest. What was she thinking? I was in a nightgown, after all, with nothing on underneath! He didn't seem to notice or care. Neither did my mom. He walked slowly toward the bed, and I stood up, arms still locked in an *X* in front of me.

"Are you well?" he asked.

"I am. In fact, I feel better than ever." It was true. I didn't have an ache or pain anywhere, and I felt more rested than I could ever remember.

"Good." He dropped his eyes and fumbled with the edges of his sleeveless cloak, drawing the two halves together over his chest. "Good," he said again, his long, dark lashes brushing his cheeks as he looked at the floor. Wow, was he cute, even though under the open cloak, he was wearing what I would call a dress — a tunic that hit him just below the knees and nicely showed off his calves.

Mom and I exchanged glances. I raised my eyebrows as if to ask, "What's up with him?" She shook her head slightly as if to say, "I don't know."

"Well, Mark, thank you for checking on Seraphina," Mom said.

For checking on me again, I added silently, remembering him standing outside the door a while ago.

"Oh, um, yes." He gestured to a basket he had set on the floor at the entrance to the room. "I'm taking food to Aunt Shayna today."

"Mmmm?" my mother asked.

Mark fiddled with the flaps of his cloak and cleared his throat. "You said you wanted me to take something to her."

My mother's hands flew up. "Oh, yes, of course! The raisin cakes! Wait one moment." She hurried from the room, and Mark looked to me.

"While you were sick, Aunt Shayna hurt her foot," he explained.

"Oh." It was all I could say. Who was Aunt Shayna, anyway?

"She can't join us tomorrow for the feast, so I am bringing her some things."

"Oh." Wow, what a brilliant conversationalist I was becoming. Thankfully, my mother came back into the room and stuffed a wrapped bundle into the basket.

"There," she said, brushing off her hands as she stood. "Thank you for reminding me, Mark. I had other things on my mind." She looked pointedly at me.

"Can I go with you?" I asked Mark. He opened his mouth to respond, but my mother jumped in instead.

"Seraphina, you have been quite ill."

"No, Mother, really, I feel fine. Could I go, please?"

She looked to Mark, who simply shrugged his shoulders.

My mother felt my forehead and pressed her fingers under my jaw to feel my glands. "No fever. No more swelling." She glanced at Mark.

"She can come with me, if she would like," he said.

My mother considered it for a moment and surprised me with her answer.

"All right. But you must not tire yourself," she said with the shake of a finger at me.

"I won't let her," Mark interjected.

"And be home for the evening meal," she said.

I opened my mouth to answer, but Mark jumped in again. "I'll see to it," he said.

"Then put on your sandals," she said to me, motioning to the floor at the end of my bed, "and don't forget your veil."

From a table next to the bed, she plucked up a length of white material — the cloth I had worn around my wet hair when I got out of the shower. How could that be? I stood paralyzed as I watched her shake it out. She positioned it on my head and tucked the loose ends in under my hair behind my neck.

"Your sandals," she said again.

I gave up being modest and uncrossed my arms. I fetched the sandals from where she pointed on the floor, then I sat on the edge of the bed. The worn straps of leather were tacked into soles that felt like wood. Upon closer inspection, I noted that they *were* wood, thinly layered. It didn't matter which foot I put into which sandal. They were identical rectangles, no left or right.

What was wrong with me? Mom was there. Mark was there. But *where* were we? If this was my home, why did this place seem so strange?

I knotted a cloth belt around my waist and walked to the door with Mark.

"Seraphina, mantle," Mom said. What was she talking about? I looked around the room. There wasn't a fireplace to be seen.

"Your mantle," she said again and pulled a woven shawl from a peg near the door. A golden zigzag design worked its way through the burgundy fabric which she settled over my shoulders.

"Now, don't be late," she cautioned. "You have chores, and if you are up to going with Mark, you are up to doing them, too. You can start by dumping the pot on your way out."

She motioned to a corner of the room. I walked over to find a large crockery bowl with a rope handle covered by a slab of wood. Next to it was a basket of leaves. I lifted the lid covering the bowl.

"Ick!" The bile backed up into my throat at the smell. It was nearly full. It was our toilet.

Mark and my mother paid no attention to me.

"The city is so crowded, we will walk outside the wall," Mark said. He looked to my mother for confirmation, and she nodded.

"I'll get some water from the cistern," he said to me as he led the way across our courtyard. He drew water from the opening in the ground and poured it into a crockery pitcher.

Carrying the pot with my arm extended as far as it would go, I followed him through the door that opened onto the street. No cars. No lamp posts. No sidewalks. Just people. And animals. Everywhere. Not my neighborhood at all.

Mark wasn't kidding about the crowding. People young and old jammed together as they slowly made their way in one direction or another, mothers desperately trying to keep their little ones close.

"All right, dump it," Mark said, motioning a bit impatiently to the pot I held.

Where? I wanted to ask, but then I noticed the gutter lined with half-pipe shaped stones. I poured out the contents of the pot, trying not to let anything splash up onto my legs. Mark "flushed," sloshing the pitcher of water down the channel, washing everything away. At least away from in front of where we stood.

We set pitcher and pot inside the door to my courtyard and merged with bodies in the street.

Dogs ran along the edges of the crowd while donkeys carried bundles and kids on their backs. And then there was a camel. No, two! They passed right in front of us, and I crouched behind Mark's shoulder in case one of them (the camels, that is) decided to spit.

It smelled like the zoo — only riper. I breathed in and out through my mouth and checked the bottoms of my sandals to make sure I hadn't stepped in anything. They were clean, but I had to watch where I walked. Squishy brown curls and larger mounds of pellets that looked like big black olives dotted the stone roadway.

As he threaded a path through the crowd, Mark grabbed my hand, and my heart skittered in my chest. I only hoped that the rough skin wouldn't gross him out.

"Jerusalem at Passover — is there a more crowded city?" he asked.

Jerusalem! I would have stopped in place, if not for the gentle pull of his hand. My head swiveled back and forth, my eyes soaking in the square-shaped, golden-colored houses stepping their way up the hillside behind us like sugar cubes, one upon another.

The people around us were all dressed in robes, and many of them sported head coverings. Most of the adults had bundles tucked under their arms, as did the older children, and some of the men held birdcages aloft, out of the way of the traffic. My ears were filled with a din of voices talking in various languages, shouting, and laughing.

Every so often, the occasional baby's wail or donkey's bray punctuated the air.

I felt as if I were having an out-of-body experience. How could I possibly be here? Was this really my home? The place was strange, but Mom and Mark were familiar. Had I lost my memory while I was sick? What was happening to me?

Something warm oozed between my toes, bringing me back to the moment. Mark waited patiently as I used a stone to scrape a dog's mess from my foot and sandal. After that, I paid better attention to where I stepped.

Ahead of us loomed the city wall constructed of row upon row of cut stone blocks stacked tens of feet tall. Along the very top, gaps as broad as a man's arm span evenly separated sections of stone the same width. They looked like widely spaced teeth running along the entire perimeter. Like the points of a crown.

Mark took my hand again and guided me through a tangle of people funneling themselves through an arched opening in the wall, most of them moving in the opposite direction from us, into the city. Even though we were headed downhill, I felt as if we were salmon swimming upstream. Finally, we emerged through the arch in the wall, leaving the noisy city behind us and entering a calmer, quieter valley.

We turned to the right and followed the road in a clockwise direction around the outside of the wall of the city. I think Mark had forgotten he was holding my hand. I wished he wouldn't remember, but he did, and he let it go and shifted the basket from one hand to the other.

"I heard you saying what it was like when you had the fever. Your dream," he said.

"Yes, but I'm not sure it was really a dream."

He cocked an eyebrow at me.

"I mean, everything here seems so strange to me," I said. "But I remember everything about that other place where I was living and everything about that time."

"It wasn't Jerusalem?" he asked.

"Oh, no," I said. "It was Amer—" I snapped my mouth shut. Surely America didn't exist for these people — yet. I wanted to say it was a country on the other side of the world, but as far as I knew, the world ended for Mark where the sea slipped off the edge of the earth. "I lived in a place far, far away. But when I woke up — I was here! I don't know how I got here, but, Mark, I think I really *was* living in another time."

He considered what I said for a few minutes, then asked, "Was I there?"

A blush burned its way across my cheeks, but luckily he kept his eyes to the road. I didn't want him to think he had been starring in my dreams. Even though he did plenty of that. But it was true. He *was* there.

"What makes you think you would be there?" I asked him.

He looked over at me and raised his shoulders. "Well, I *am* your brother."

I stopped dead in my tracks, and he walked on a few paces before he realized I wasn't at his side, and then he stopped.

My brother? No way! *Steven* was my brother, not Mark. I couldn't have a crush on my brother!

It took a moment for me to wrap my brain around what he had actually said. When I finally did, I sighed with relief as I realized that the Aramaic word he had used for "brother" was *aha*, which could also mean kinsman. Thank goodness! We may have been in the same clan or tribe or something, but at least he wasn't my *brother* brother.

"You were my neighbor," I said when I caught up to him.

He chuckled. "Things don't change much. We've been neighbors all our lives."

So he knew me forever. In this place. Just as I knew him — back home.

"Sera—" He watched the dust puff up around his feet as we walked. "Even if you can't remember some things, I'm glad you are feeling better."

Physically, yes. But mentally? I wasn't sure. "I'm glad that doctor was there," I said.

"Doctor? Oh, Yeshua. He is quite the healer."

"You know him?" I asked.

Mark looked at me as if to say, "Are you nuts?"

"We both do," he said slowly, confused by my confusion. "And, yes, he healed you."

"Mark, it was more than that. I was . . ." I stopped. "He brought me back."

His eyes glistened with tears. "I know. I've seen it before."

"You have?"

"His work is . . . amazing. I still can't get used to what he can do, even after being with him these many months. Watching him in Bethany . . . and seeing Lazarus . . . and . . ."

I jerked to a halt and latched my hand around Mark's bicep. "Yeshua? Yeshua — Jesus?" I asked.

"Yes — "

It couldn't be. It wasn't possible, was it? "What's the date?" I asked, my heart thundering under my ribs. "It's not 33, is it?"

"Thirty-three what?"

"The year. Is the year 33?"

Mark cocked his head, and an inverted *V* etched itself between his eyebrows. He lifted his hand to touch my forehead, checking for recurring fever, I'm sure.

"I'm fine." I took his hand in mine. "Really, I'm fine. For some reason, I just can't remember the year." He didn't pull his fingers away. Instead, they closed gently on my hand.

"It is the seventeenth year of the Emperor Tiberius."

Oh, great. That helped a lot. Exactly when *was* that? Something about the way Mark said it was vaguely familiar. Wasn't there a bit in the Bible about the reign of the Emperor Tiberius? But where? Old Testament? New? I was not only out of place, I was lost in time, but in a time that was somehow still mine.

CHAPTER FIVE

We walked in silence for many moments while thoughts collided inside my head. Was I a first-century Jew named Seraphina who dreamt she had lived two thousand years in the future? Or was I a twenty-first-century American girl called Ronni cast back into the time of Jesus? My temples ached from trying to sort it out.

And the excitement gushed through my veins. Jesus! He had saved me. Touched me. Healed me! He was real, alive, here! I stopped walking. He *was* alive, but for how long?

I continued to shuffle along as, slowly, realization dawned: I had knowledge no one else around me had. I knew what was coming, what the people here would face. I knew that Jesus would be killed — but things didn't have to be that way, did they? *Nothing is worth dying for*, I thought. If Jesus could be saved, if he lived, how much more good could he do? How many more people would come to believe in him?

But should I stop the crucifixion? What would that do to God's plan of salvation? Could I possibly stop Jesus' death? I had no idea how. And when would it happen? This year? Next? I racked my brain trying to think of how I could find out exactly where I was in history.

"Mark," I began tentatively, "because of the fever, my memory has holes in it. Can you help me?"

"I will try."

Okay, this was it. I'd just have to take a stab in the dark. "I remember bits and pieces of things. Like Yeshua riding on a donkey. People lining the road with their cloaks and waving palm branches. Am I crazy?"

He turned to face me, a crooked smile playing on his lips. "No. You were there." He laughed. "You were yelling louder than anyone."

"Hosanna?" I asked.

"That, and more."

I chewed my lower lip, trying to picture myself as part of that raucous mob. "When did this happen?"

"On the first day of the week." I wrinkled my brow at that information. "Three days ago," he added helpfully.

How could that be? I distinctly remembered Palm Sunday and sitting at home after Mass trying to recall how Dad used to fold and tuck the palm fronds into crosses. He never went to Mass with us, but he had a real knack for making those crosses each year. Last Sunday's Gospel told of Jesus' entry into Jerusalem. Is that why it was fresh in my mind? I couldn't possibly have been at home making crosses *and* here waving palms, could I?

But I *was* here — now. And this was Wednesday. That meant that on Friday . . . Two days. That's all I had. "Where do you think Yeshua is right now?" I asked.

"Probably teaching in the Temple," Mark answered. "That is, if they'll let him anywhere near the place after what he did there. And if it's still standing. Yesterday he said that the Temple would be destroyed. Can you believe it? 'Not one stone will be left upon another,' he said."

"Yes, I heard about it." I'd listened to those words being read from the Gospel my whole life. "Can we go there? To the Temple? I'd like to thank him," I said. But, really, I wanted to do so much more than that.

"We'll go right after I deliver this." He lifted the basket in front of my face, and the aroma of something spicy hooked my nostrils. My stomach gurgled. That fig I'd eaten wasn't going to last me very long, I could tell.

We continued to circle the outside of the city clockwise along its western edge until the road began to curve away into open country. Mark turned off from the lane that would take us that way and directed me toward the city, to the hill propping up the wall that was set high on top of it.

"Where are we going?" I asked.

He didn't answer; he just led the way along a footpath drawing closer to the hill. He rounded a bend, and I stopped. Whitewashed rectangles dotted the slope, glinting in the bright sunshine. We had entered a graveyard. But these graves weren't dug into the ground; instead, they were elevated horizontal stone enclosures that reminded me of concrete coffins. Farther back, dug into the hillside were cave-like openings that must have been additional burial places.

Mark carefully skirted the tombs, stopped at one of the raised rectangles, and stood back a respectable distance. This tomb was bigger than most of the others. Big enough for two, I realized, and the engraving on the slab confirmed whose grave this was.

"I miss you," Mark said, so quietly I could barely hear it. "I'll never forget you, Steven Bar Samuel."

Steven, son of Samuel. My brother. My father. Buried here together. I took a step closer to the grave, my hands stretching to touch it, but Mark grabbed my arm.

"What are you doing?" he asked as he jerked me back. "Don't touch! You'll be unclean. You won't be able to celebrate Passover."

"Says who?" I asked.

"The Pharisees. It is the law. You know that."

"I won't touch," I said, but he raised his eyebrows in skepticism. "I promise. I just want to be near them."

He released my arm, and I knelt down next to the grave, careful not to touch it. I leaned over the smooth stone surface and inhaled the whitewash made from chemical-smelling lime. Tears plopped onto the slab. The loss wrenched my heart as if it had happened yesterday. Mark stood back and left me to my sorrow for several minutes, but then he placed his hand softly on my shoulder.

"Come," he said. He bent down and helped me to my feet.

"Thank you," I whispered to him. Despite my sadness and confusion, I felt a sense of comfort in knowing that Steven and Dad were here with me, even if I didn't know how or why I was in Jerusalem.

Mark led me away, guiding me between the graves, careful not to touch them. He walked so close to me that his arm brushed mine with every step he took.

My tears blurred the path in front of me. "They died for nothing, didn't they?"

Mark shrugged and kept his head down, but a moment later he stole a sideways glance at me.

"What?" I asked.

"At least they are in good company here," he said.

"What do you mean?"

He jerked his head at me as an invitation to follow him. We left the graveyard and continued closer to the hill that formed the foundation of the city. Its steep grade was arrested at the bottom where the hill met the valley. It was as if a giant animal had taken a huge bite out of the slope. And at its base, there gaped a wide, deep pit.

It was a rock quarry. I'd seen one once before in the Colorado mountains, but where that one had given up its granite, this one yielded limestone. The yellow-gold blocks that had built Jerusalem must have come from this quarry.

"You wouldn't know it by looking at it, would you?" Mark asked.

"Know what?"

"They say that Adam is buried here. Beneath the hill."

"Adam who? Oh, *Adam*. Here? Really?" I wanted to laugh. I mean, how could they possibly know that?

"It has been long believed." His eyes traced the outline of the massive hill, and his seriousness sobered me. "It would make sense. This *is* a holy mountain. Part of the range of Moriah."

My face registered puzzlement.

A wry smile washed over his face. "Where Abraham took Isaac."

"To sacrifice him," I added.

"Where he showed his faithfulness to God. He named this place 'the Lord will provide.' Is it any wonder that this became David's city or that our Temple is built on this hill?" His face beamed with pride and affection.

"Then I guess it's not that hard to think of Adam being buried here," I said.

We walked through the quarry where massive slabs were stacked in front of the sheared-off wall. "What's with that part?" I pointed to a section along the base of the cliff. The limestone had been exposed, but the scoring marks were uneven, and here and there chunks had fallen away.

Mark and I walked closer to it. "It's too soft. They tried to quarry it, but it just crumbled. It's no good for building, so they abandoned this section. They took the blocks for the Temple from over there." He pointed to an adjacent site.

We left the quarry, walked a little farther, and entered a gate at the northern edge of the city. The crowds were as thick at this end of Jerusalem as they had been in our neighborhood. After a few minutes of weaving our way through people and animals, we entered Mark's aunt's home.

"Come in, children, come in!" Aunt Shayna, hobbling on a make-shift cane, beckoned us to sit on the floor at her low table. It took both of us to help lower her down. Mark set the basket in front of her, and she happily dug through its contents and smiled with a mouthful of crooked, yellow teeth, of which I guessed about half were missing.

"Thank you for bringing this," she said to Mark as she pulled him toward her for a kiss. He blushed mightily, but he let her do her thing before he stood up.

"I'll be right back." He slipped through the door, leaving me alone with the aunt.

I cleared my throat. "So, how did you hurt yourself?" I asked. It was the last thing I said for about five minutes as she launched into a long story about tripping on a dog and falling on the Temple steps, or stepping on a dog on the way to the Temple, or walking with her dog to visit the Temple, or something. I really couldn't follow her. I just nodded and smiled and said a consoling "mmm" at the appropriate times. I kept stealing glances at the door, impatient for Mark's return and eager to leave so we could find Jesus.

She stopped for a breath, and I jumped in to ask if I could take a look at her foot. If I was going to have to wait, I might as well make myself useful. She dumped her heel into my lap and pulled up her skirt just enough for me to see her grapefruit-sized purple ankle.

"Can you move your toes?" I asked. She could. "Flex your foot?" Yes. My coach had me do those things when I wrenched my ankle in soccer last year. "I think it's just sprained . . . uh, twisted." I remembered what I had learned about taking care of a sprain: R.I.C.E. Rest, ice, compression, elevation.

"You really should stay off of it. Keep it higher than your heart. And put ice on it." She laughed at that, then so did I. Where could you get ice in Jerusalem in springtime — or ever?

"Well, keep it up at least." I settled her onto a cot and propped her foot onto some rolled-up blankets. "This should help," I said as I wrapped long strips of cloth around the swollen joint to immobilize her foot. "Now try to stay off this for the next couple of days. I'm sure Mark will check in with you."

Mark. Where was he?

I opened the door to see him on the opposite side of the street . . . and being hugged by a girl. Adrenaline shot to my temples. The girl had her back to me, but even from this angle, she looked like a princess in her white dress capped by a navy blue shawl. Her blonde hair was braided around the top of her head like a crown. People passing by shot them some disapproving looks. I gathered that PDAs were not acceptable here.

The girl released Mark, slid her hands down his arms, and clasped his hands in hers. Mark lifted his head, a huge grin lighting up his face. A lump the size of a golf ball lodged in the back of my throat. He saw me then, and said something to the girl. She turned to face me, and my jaw hit the ground. Tabby. So that's how things were here. Maybe that's the way they'd always been.

CHAPTER SIX

Mark and Tabby didn't seem to mind my seeing them in that bear hug. And why should they? I'd never told Tabby how I felt about Mark, and as far as Mark was concerned, I was just his friend's little sister. I didn't have a claim on him. Then or now. That was all too clear.

As they walked up to me, the two of them switched from speaking Latin, of which I understood only little, to Greek, which I could actually follow. This first-century me was way smarter than the twenty-first-century version.

"You're better!" Tabby said, clasping my hands in hers. "I'm glad."

"Yeah. Thanks." I pulled my hands from hers.

"Are you ready to go?" Mark asked me.

"Yes." I poked my head into his aunt's small home to say goodbye, but she was fast asleep. I pulled the door shut behind me.

"Where are the two of you going?" Tabby asked.

"To the Temple. To see the Rabbi Yeshua," Mark answered.

Tabby snorted. "Oh, him. He's a troublemaker, my father says."

"No, Tabitha, he's not," Mark said. "He's a peacemaker. Come with us. Just listen to him."

I wrinkled my nose at that suggestion. I didn't exactly want her along, but she agreed to come and fell into step next to me.

We threaded our way through people, turned down a lane or two, then crested a hill in the street, and I froze in my tracks. Up ahead, the Temple loomed, bigger than I could have ever imagined. It looked as if at least twenty soccer fields could fit within it. The late afternoon sun splashed across the golden façade that glistened as if honey-drizzled.

"Seraphina, come on. Seraphina? What is it?" Mark asked.

"Nothing. Everything. It's so beautiful."

"Well, I can't argue with that," Tabby said. "But if you ask me, all that sacrificing seems a bit much."

At the mention of sacrificing, a whiff of something burning wafted to me. It was a scent made up of several different smells, all working together like notes in a symphony. The melody line, however, was the roasting of meat, and my stomach answered its song with a loud rumble. A spiral of smoke curled upward, puffing from the Temple like incense from the censer I held when serving a solemn Mass.

"You Romans sacrifice to your gods, too," Mark said. "Sacrificing is part of our history, but not the most important thing."

"Oh, really?" Tabby asked. "And what is?"

"I heard Yeshua say that to love God with all your heart, and your neighbor as yourself, is a greater thing than all the Temple sacrifices," he answered.

"Which god, though?" she asked defiantly.

"Ah, you Romans have many idols, but they are just stone or wood," Mark answered. "Ours is the one, true God. A living God. He created all things. He gives life."

"A living god?" she asked. "Like a real person?"

"Well, yes," I said. "God is our Father. Because he loves us, he sent his Son to live as a man among us. Yeshua."

Tabby knit her brow as she tried to absorb what I'd said, and even Mark had a look on his face that let me know he didn't quite get it all, either.

"Uh, let's go in," I said. I didn't want to be explaining doctrine to Tabby and Mark right now. It was weird to know more than they did.

We entered a large stone-paved area ringing the Temple. "Yeshua often teaches here in the Gentiles' Court," Mark said, "but I don't see him." I didn't see much of anything except for the backs of the people in front of me.

A low wall separated the courtyard from the Temple itself. "You go on in," Tabby offered. "I'll wait here for you." She moved to the side, and I caught my breath. There, engraved into a large stone block in seven lines of Greek text was a very clear message:

NO GENTILE
MAY ENTER WITHIN THE BARRICADE
WHICH SURROUNDS THE SANCTUARY AND ENCLOSURE
WHOEVER IS CAUGHT DOING SO
WILL HAVE HIMSELF TO BLAME
FOR HIS DEATH
WHICH WILL FOLLOW

Tabby couldn't come in. She was a Roman living in Jerusalem. A Gentile. If Yeshua had been in the Gentiles' Court where we had been standing, Tabby could have heard him. As it was, Mark and I left her behind and walked up a set of stairs, through an arch, and into the Women's Court, which I could see was open to men as well. At the far end, another set of stairs climbed to a magnificent entryway flanked by two huge pillars on each side. I imagined that girls couldn't go beyond that point since only men were climbing the steps.

"Oh, good. They're going to start," Mark said.

"Who?"

"The Levite choir. Let's see if we can get closer."

The crowd grew tighter together around me, but if I jumped up and down, I could catch a glimpse of the men gathered at the top of the staircase. They began to sing a psalm in Hebrew, and even though I could catch only the occasional phrase because of the bustle of activity all around me, I knew what the words meant.

O Lord, thou God of vengeance, thou God of vengeance, shine forth!
Rise up, O judge of the earth; render to the proud what they deserve!
O Lord, how long shall the wicked, how long shall the wicked exult?

My neck craned upward as far as it would go, eyes taking in the columns, the parapets, and the balconies ringing the court. On either side of me, people jostled and joked, argued and elbowed their way through the crowd. We were being carried along in a sea of bodies. Mark bumped into me, I lost my footing, stumbled away from him, and flung out my arms to grab something — anything — before I fell and was trampled to death. My palms landed on a pair of forearms, the fingers of my right hand grasping a small black calfskin box bound to the man's left arm with a leather strap. It took only a moment to realize what it was. A phylactery. And there was a matching one attached to his forehead.

When our religion class read Matthew's Gospel, Mr. Josephson had explained what a phylactery was, and I tried to imagine what the boxes containing Scripture passages looked like. And here was one right now, worn by a real-life Pharisee in fine clothing with extra-long tassels hanging from the corners of his colorful prayer shawl. A Pharisee whose face was contorted in horror as he stared at my arms on his.

My eyes followed his to the crusty, oozing patches on the backs of my hands. He drew himself away, pointed toward me, and began yelling, "Unclean, unclean!"

"No, no," I tried to assure him, but he backed up a step, drawing his robes across his chest to protect himself from contamination.

Like a receding tide, the crowd pulled back and fanned out into a circle around us as the Pharisee continued shouting at me, "Unclean!" Women stretched corners of their mantles over their mouths and noses and drew their children close. Mark's face was deep in the crowd at this point, but he was frantically trying to bulldoze his way to me.

"Call the guard," the Pharisee ordered to no one in particular. "Call the Temple guard! Take her to the Lepers' Court."

"It's not leprosy!" I yelled. "Eczema. Eczema. Don't you know anything?"

Apparently not. A moment later, a bearded giant with greasy, pitch-black hair sticking out from under what looked like a leather helmet muscled his way through the crowd. Capping his eyes were thick, dark brows shaped like huge triangles that could just as well have been arrows or horns. He held a long baton of smooth wood that I knew he had no intention of twirling. He smacked it into his open palm like a Chicago cop in an old-time gangster movie.

"Take her to the priests," the Pharisee ordered. Arrow Brows poked the pole into my stomach with such force that the air whooshed from my lungs, and I doubled over. The crowd parted, and I back-pedaled until my backside smacked into the wall.

"No, you can't!" I begged, gasping for air. "You don't know what you're doing!"

The Pharisee's jaw clenched and his cheeks reddened. "How dare you speak thus to me," he snarled, his lips barely moving. "A female. And a child at that!"

I'm not a child! I wanted to scream at him. Girls my age married here. You could see them everywhere carrying babies and bundles and following their husbands along the streets. But to this fossil of a Pharisee, everyone probably seemed young. And women here apparently didn't engage men in talk. I shut my mouth.

Mark had finally made it to the center of the circle, and he began pleading with the Pharisee. Arrow Brows turned to face Mark, all the while pinning me to the wall with the baton.

"She's not unclean," I heard Mark explain. "Please don't exile her to the leper colony." Arrow Brows glanced back to make sure I wasn't going anywhere, then turned back, and with the Pharisee, he launched into argument with Mark.

"Seraphina!" Tabitha's head poked around the corner of the wall, her shawl drawn up over her hair and across her face. I inhaled sharply. What was she doing there? Committing suicide? If they found her in there . . . She gestured for me to follow her. I shook my head wildly and mouthed, "Go away!" But she set her jaw, swung her head from side to side, and motioned again for me to come. If she didn't get out quickly, she'd be spotted soon.

I sucked in my stomach, inched back from the baton, and with my fingers behind my hips, felt my way along the wall. No one in the crowd noticed, so intent were they on the three-way argument. The Pharisee and the guard both had their backs to me, but Mark didn't. With a flick of his eyes in my direction, he acknowledged my escape-in-progress.

Tabby's arm snaked around the corner and hooked my elbow. "Hurry," she hissed. I let her pull me from the Women's Court and through the arch. Dodging people as best we could, we raced across the Court of the Gentiles and down the steps, taking them two at a time. A roar from behind us announced that my escape had been detected.

"Run!" Mark's shout came from far off. Tabby pulled me away from the Temple and down a wide street, past stall after stall overflowing with cheeses for sale.

"Faster!" Mark was closer now, and I chanced a look over my shoulder. His swift strides closed the gap between us, but not all that far behind him, Arrow Brows and two others plowed through people in the street. Mark snatched a small, round cheese from a table and rifled it at Arrow Brows like a catcher throwing out a runner stealing second base. The cheese smacked the guard right in the gut, but he kept on running. At a narrowing in the road, Mark knocked over a couple of carts filled with woven baskets. Surely that would slow the men down. It did, for maybe a nanosecond.

Mark caught up to us and dragged us past perplexed people and around vendors' tables where weavers, potters, and metalworkers displayed their goods for the Passover crowd. We zigzagged down alleyways and around small homes and shops. When I chanced a look, I couldn't see Arrow Brows behind us, but I was certain he was still there.

The gray stone wall of the city was now visible on my left, high and thick, impossible to scale. Up in front of us, the street dead-ended at a large pool of water, a public bath or reservoir of some sort. It seemed we were out of escape options.

"Where are we?" I screamed.

"The Pool of Siloam," he answered.

I twirled in a circle, trying to figure a way out. Spotting a narrow lane emerging from between two houses, I made a move toward it, but Mark snagged my arm.

"Wait!" he commanded. "There — go through Hezekiah's Tunnel." He pointed to the far end of the pool where an archway yawned, revealing nothing but blackness beyond the entrance.

"You've . . . got . . . to be . . . kidding!" I gasped, holding my aching side.

He wasn't. Stairs led down to the water, and he raced down them and rushed along the near edge of the pool with Tabby and me trailing him. A lighted torch flanked either side of the arch. He pulled one from its bracket and thrust it at me before slogging across the pool, yanking the other out of its support, and dunking it into the water where it hissed out. "You'll need the light, and if those guards follow, at least *they* won't be able to see."

He splashed his way back to our side of the pool. I tried to draw in enough air to plead with him. "Mark, listen, I don't think —"

"Shush!" he ordered. "No time to argue. I'll go outside the wall and meet you at the exit. You'll have to hurry, because if they figure out what you've done, they'll be there, too."

"Wait!" Tabitha said. She ripped the mantle from my shoulders.

"Hey, what —" I started to say, but Tabby ignored me.

She took off her own shawl, wadded it up, and stuffed it into her belt. She draped my mantle over her head, completely covering her blonde hair, and drew it across her face so that only her eyes were visible. "They'll be looking for Seraphina to be wearing this," she said to Mark. "Maybe I can distract them."

"Smart," Mark said. "But be careful. You're putting yourself in danger."

Her blue eyes grew as big as Frisbees, but she just nodded.

"Wait until you see them come near the pool," he said. "Make sure they see Seraphina's mantle on you. Then run away through that lane. Go quickly to where the road turns to the right. My cousin Barnabas lives in the last house on the lane. He will hide you. But don't let those guards catch you. I'll hide and watch from here. If it looks as if you're in trouble, I'll stop them."

She lifted her chin slightly and looked from him to me. "They won't catch me." She pulled the ends of my mantle tight over her chest, completely hiding her shawl, and sprinted away from the pool, up the steps two at a time. She was gone before I could say anything. Before I could stop her, warn her . . . thank her.

"Now, go!" Mark said, shoving me toward the gaping hole of darkness.

"But the opening is so small," I said.

"You will be fine, *sivnapi*," he said, pronouncing it *sin'-a-pee*. Mustard seed.

I bent over and, with my free hand, reached between my ankles and grabbed a handful of the back of my skirt. Pulling it through my legs, I tucked it into the front of my belt, hiking the fabric out of reach of the water. Anyone who saw my bare legs would surely be scandalized, but I didn't care. I kicked off my sandals and tucked them into my belt, too, then ducking my head, I splashed into the tunnel from which water was running to fill the pool. I felt as if I were being devoured by a snake. Where exactly *would* I come out? It certainly wouldn't be the Emerald City, and if this was the Yellow Brick Road I was walking on, it sure was cold and wet.

"You can do it," Mark shouted at me. "Just like David."

I looked back at the shrinking hole of daylight behind me. But he was already gone.

Oh, great. Did he mean David, the one who offed Goliath? Well, I wasn't facing Goliath . . . or was I? It didn't matter. David had divine help. And then it occurred to me that I could have that help, too. "Father, please guide me!" I prayed, and the darkness covered me like a blanket, punctuated only by the torch's light.

CHAPTER SEVEN

Large potholes pitted the floor of the tunnel, and depending on how flat a particular section was, the water ranged from just grazing my ankles to covering my knees. And it was chilly. After a few minutes, numbness sapped all feeling from my feet.

The rough-hewn walls narrowed in places to barely a body width, and sometimes the ceiling was so low that I had to bend over. I kept my arm locked straight in front of me, holding the torch like a light saber.

The scent of minerals hung in a passageway so humid that my hair began to frizz and droplets gathered on my face. Or was that sweat? Every once in a while, something slimy slithered past my feet, and I wondered if rats called this black tunnel home. Make that cold sweat.

I tried not to think about how far underground I was, because when I did, claustrophobia crept up my back, and my breath chugged from my lungs in shortened puffs. My fingers itched something horribly, and I alternated the hand that held the torch so that I could rub the eczema patches against the fabric of my shift. The only relief I could get was to dunk them into the cold water, but that meant crouching down, and walking like that slowed me down.

I calmed myself and continued marching on, despite the disgusting possibility of rodents, despite the irritating itch of my hands, despite the fact that if I was caught, something awful was going to happen to me.

Then the torch sputtered, showering me in sparks. Too little oxygen? No, a breeze brushed past my cheeks, but it wasn't blowing strongly enough to extinguish the fire. The torch was burning out. There just wasn't enough fuel left. I felt like one of the bridesmaids in Jesus' parable — the ones who didn't bring extra oil for their torches. The thing I held looked like the Wicked Witch's broom, burnt to a crisp down to the handle after Dorothy tossed a bucket of water on it. As that thought finished forming in my mind, the torch went out. Blackness. Everywhere.

"No! No!" My voice bounced off the walls and landed shrilly in my ears. I stopped walking and slammed the useless torch into the water, splashing my clothing. My feet were popsicles, my will equally frozen. I couldn't dam up the tears.

"Stop it, stop it," I told myself, knowing I had to quit crying if I hoped to get out of that mess. But I couldn't stop crying completely. It was darker than anything I had ever experienced. My pupils must be huge, black holes, I thought. A match! That would have helped. Or a hundred matches.

Wait! The light from my cell phone! I had gone so far as to put my hand on a pocket I didn't have before reality jerked me back. I had no cell phone. No matches. No help.

I mulled over my choices. I could stand there and wait for someone to find me — not Arrow Brows, I hoped. Or I could try to get out on my own. I didn't want to go back and risk what I might find waiting for me there. The only thing that made sense was to push on.

I curved my arms in front of my head, the right one slightly higher so I didn't smash my forehead into a stalagmite. Or was that stalactite? I should have paid more attention in science class. Which-ever was the one that hangs down from the ceiling in a cave, I didn't want to meet it head-on.

Something splashed up ahead of me. It sounded big and rat-like. Panic shot through me. I stopped walking and braced a foot on each side of the wall to lift myself out of the water, hoping that the thing would float downstream under the bridge of my legs.

More splashes. *Must be a whole rat family*, I thought, shuddering. The tunnel was filled with a high-pitched squeal. Mine.

"Seraphina?"

"Mark, Mark is that you?" I jumped back into the water and moved as quickly as I could, my hands outstretched until they met something solid.

"Ouch!"

"What happened?" I said.

"You poked me in the eye."

"Sorry." My arms were on his then, and nothing had ever felt so secure.

He turned around, trailing one arm in back for me to hang on to. "We're not far," he said, and it seemed like only minutes before the tunnel gradually lightened.

The exit was a narrow gap which opened onto a spring that sent water into the tunnel and eventually filled the pool. Mark squeezed out, and I followed him, emerging from the tunnel into the sunlit day.

"Do you think Tabitha made it home?" I asked. "Did they follow her?" Or were they coming to get me? I swung my head around, but couldn't spot Arrow Brows or his pals. I wished I knew if Tabby had made it okay. She really came through for me, and I felt the heavy burden of guilt settle on my shoulders. I hadn't treated her all that nicely, and she had risked her life for me. What if something had happened to her? If ever there was a time for cell phones, this was it.

"Don't worry. They're not here," Mark said. "You're safe. And I'm sure Tabitha is, too."

So he read my mind. Or else he was concerned like I was. "I hope so," I said. "You really care about her, don't you? I mean, I saw that hug."

He looked at me sideways from the corner of his eye, and the right side of his lips jerked up into that crooked half-smile of his. "She sat with you while you were sick, you know."

No, I didn't know. "Really?"

"Uh-huh. She left just before Yeshua got there. She didn't know you were better until I told her. *That's* why she was hugging me."

Where was a hole I could climb into? I looked back to the opening to the spring, wishing I could disappear into it again.

"She was really worried about you. And when I told her about how you thought you lived in the future . . ."

"You what?" I asked.

Redness flushed at his neck and crept up into his face. "Sorry."

I crossed my arms in front of me and with my toe, chipped away at a dried dirt clod on the ground. "She must think I'm insane," I said.

"No, she doesn't. She understands what a fever can do."

I didn't know whether to be mad or grateful. To hear him tell my story, I had to admit, it *did* sound a bit out-there. But I was sure it was true. I knew all about that time in the faraway future. And the things to come in the very near future.

Gray clouds moved in to shutter the sun, and a brisk wind chilled my wet skin. I pulled my sandals from my belt and shoved my feet into them as I untucked my gown. Much of it was drenched. Great. I'd come home soaking wet . . . and without my mantle. Mom was going to kill me. What was I talking about? Maybe I was already dead and this was part of my afterlife.

"You're shivering." Mark took off his sleeveless cloak, and I poked my arms into the wide arm holes.

"Thanks." I looked back to the tiny opening from which we had popped. "David didn't really do what I just did, did he?"

"Yes. Either David or his men. Or both. Only they went in the opposite direction. From out here into the city. And there wasn't a tunnel yet."

"Then how did he do it?" I asked.

"He went in there," Mark pointed to the spring's entrance. "And climbed a vertical shaft."

"But why?"

"To get in. To defeat the Jebusites," he said. "To conquer Zion and make this *his* city."

"Well, lucky for me he knew this shortcut. And lucky you remembered it."

We picked our way down the hill's slope, skidding on loose rocks and side-stepping prickly cactus-like patches. Mark's cloak was so long that it dragged on the ground even though I tried to keep it hiked up. But that was only half the problem. The thing was so big that it kept slipping off one shoulder, then the other. The hem picked up burrs that scraped my legs and made me stop time and again to pull them off the cloth. My ankles were raked raw when I decided I'd had enough.

"Wait a minute," I said. "I've got an idea."

I removed my cloth belt and asked Mark to hold it. Then I selected the two biggest burrs I could find, almost as large as ping-pong balls. I dug them into the fabric on my left shoulder, took the right-hand side of the cloak, pulled it across my chest, and pressed it against the burrs.

"Instant Velcro," I said, taking my belt back from Mark who looked at me with his head cocked like a curious puppy. I tied the belt around my waist and bloused the excess material over it. "Now I can walk."

"Clever girl," he said, nodding approvingly at my makeshift fasteners. "But what's Velcro?"

I laughed. "Nothing. I'm just being silly."

We picked our way down the slope in silence. I replayed in my mind everything that had happened since I woke up in Jerusalem. Something was gnawing at me, but I wasn't exactly sure how to approach it with Mark.

"I don't understand something," I began tentatively. Mark kept his eyes focused on the hillside but grunted, which I took to mean: *Well, what is it?*

I cleared my throat. "At the tombs earlier. You warned me not to touch so that I wouldn't become unclean."

"Uh-huh?" he said.

"And that Pharisee thought my touching him would make him unclean . . . because of my skin."

"Yes."

I stopped walking, and he did, too, just slightly below me on the slope. He turned to face me eye to eye. My heart fluttered, but I kept my face composed.

"But you're not afraid to touch me. You don't think that touching me makes you unclean, do you?"

He settled his eyes on his hands where he picked at dirt underneath his thumbnail.

"Do you?" I asked again.

He met my gaze. "No." To prove his point, he tugged on a ringlet of my hair that had escaped my veil, lengthening it from my shoulder to half-way down my back before letting it go to spring back up. "And I don't think that touching the dead makes me unclean either. Yeshua lays his hands on the bleeding, on the dying . . . on the dead. His touch makes them clean, whole, alive. They don't make him unclean. He told us once that it is what comes out of a man that makes him unclean. Not what goes in. Or what he touches."

"Then why didn't you let me touch the tomb?"

He hunched up one shoulder. "Because others could see. You saw what happened in the Temple. You know how the Pharisees are. I did not want you to put yourself at risk."

I nodded in understanding, and we continued down the slope.

"The Pharisees take the law too literally," he added. "They build fences around the law so no one will even come close to breaking it."

"What do you mean?" I asked.

"They make restrictions that are more severe than the actual law, so people don't get anywhere near to violating the law. But their restrictions are too much. And if I agreed with them, I would not have given you my cloak to wear."

I looked at him quizzically. He raised his eyebrow at me and quoted, "A woman must not wear men's clothing, nor a man wear women's clothing."

How could anyone remember all those rules of the law? I shook my head, gathered his cloak more closely about me, and continued downward.

At the bottom of the hill, we followed the valley until we reached the road and merged with the smattering of travelers still entering the city that late in the day. We approached a grove of fig trees where our path met up with another road. Soft green leaves covered silver branches and sheltered clusters of small, newly emerging figs. The trees waved healthy branches in the breeze. All but one. That tree appeared scorched, but no sign of fire showed in the grass at its base.

The main trunk divided into two arms stretching skyward, almost begging heaven for forgiveness. A smattering of bare boughs extended from these main branches and scratched against the sky like fingers clawing for freedom. Below the tree more dead limbs littered the ground.

"What happened here?" I asked.

"He cursed it."

"Yeshua?"

Mark nodded and picked up a branch from the ground. "He was hungry. This tree had no figs." He tossed the branch down. "Now it never will."

"But that doesn't mean it can't be useful," I said.

"What do you mean?"

"I have an idea." I searched the pile of branches and selected a five-foot length that split into a V at the end where two limbs had grown from the one. "Help me find another one like this."

Mark dug through the branches until he came up with one similarly shaped. "What do you want them for?"

"It's a surprise. I'll show you tomorrow."

Mark shouldered the two pieces of wood like a minuteman marching with his musket, and we continued on toward the city gate.

"Sorry you weren't able to find Yeshua in the Temple," Mark said.

"It's all right," I said, but it really wasn't. Just knowing he was here, and I was here, and he had healed me without my knowing who he was — it really bugged me that I hadn't found him.

When I was little, I used to wish that I had lived when Jesus did. I would fantasize about helping spread the word about the kingdom of heaven. Helping others to see who he is.

When had I lost sight of that? Where had that faith gone? I didn't need someone to answer that for me. I knew. It had died with Dad and Steven.

". . . if you wanted to go," Mark said.

"What? I'm sorry, what did you say?"

"Where were you?" he asked. "You looked as if you were far away."

I *am* far away, I wanted to tell him. "No, I was right here."

"I asked if you wanted to try to catch up with Yeshua. He has been spending the nights in Bethany." Mark gestured to the road that intersected with ours and ran off to the east.

Of course! He'd be staying with Mary, Martha . . . and Lazarus. I was about to beg him to take me when he glanced up at the sun and measured its distance above the horizon as less than a hand's width.

"It's later than I thought," he said. "We had better not. I promised your mother I'd have you home by mealtime."

"But —"

"You will see him soon," Mark said with certainty. I wasn't positive about that. What I *did* know was that if Mark wouldn't take me to him now, I would have to try to find him on my own. First thing tomorrow. There wasn't much time left.

CHAPTER EIGHT

At the entrance to my home, Mark touched the small case mounted on the doorframe, then kissed his fingers. In religion class, Mr. Josephson had told us about these little boxes attached to Jewish homes. He even showed us one that he had brought back from the Holy Land. The box contained a small scroll called the *mezuzah* — the hand-printed word of God which was to be obeyed, taught to the children, and fastened to the doorframes of houses as constant reminders.

The Scripture passage from Deuteronomy was the same as that in the phylacteries I had seen the Pharisee wearing. *Hear, O Israel: The LORD our God is one LORD! You shall love the LORD your God with all your heart, with all your soul, and with all your might.* That was all I could remember, but it was enough. I copied Mark's action and followed him into the courtyard.

"Where shall I put these?" he asked, holding out the branches.

I took them from him and propped them against the edge of the cistern. "Thanks. If you'll be visiting your aunt tomorrow, I'd like to go along." He didn't answer right away, and I wondered if maybe he was getting a little bit tired of me.

"If you don't want to, I understand," I added quickly.

"It's just that there's a lot to do tomorrow. Passover. My parents need my help."

"Oh, right."

"I guess we could go first thing in the morning," he suggested.

"That would be great! Thank you. And thank you for your help today." I made a move to give him a hug, but he had begun to turn away, and I thought better of it.

"I'll see you tomorrow," he said, and before I knew it, he was out the door.

"Seraphina, you're back!" My mother emerged from a room, the front of which was mostly open to the outside. Smoke curling into the courtyard accompanied by a delicious smell told me this was the kitchen. "Are you well?"

"Yes, Mother. I feel fine," I said, hoping she wouldn't notice my wet hem. "Will we be eating soon?" I hoped the answer was yes.

"Not much longer. I want to finish this spinning first." She nodded at the bags of wool gathered around the stool. Sitting down, she picked up the long stick that had what looked like a stone donut on the end of it. The contraption was a hand spindle, I discovered, watching Mom twirl the stick as she held it upright against the floor. She drew bits of wool from a pile that rested in her lap, and as if by magic, added fiber to the ever-lengthening strand of yarn wrapping itself around the stick.

"Mother, may I have some of that wool? I'm working on something."

Keeping her eyes on her work, she nodded, and I dug into one of the bags for a couple of fistfuls of the soft, slightly oily-feeling fiber. "Don't forget to do the milking," she said as she spun the growing length of wool through her fingers. "Then draw some water, please."

Just inside the courtyard entrance was what I guessed was a barn. The goat bleated a welcome when I poked my head in, and a handful of chickens clucked away inside a crude henhouse. Tools lined the walls, and a cart was parked in the corner. The first-century equivalent of a garage.

I walked in, and the goat set to nonstop bleating. Right. The milking. "Okay, Toto," I said to her. "Let's see if I can make this work."

I sat on the ground next to her and fetched a nearby bucket. My initial attempts at milking her didn't produce a drop, and it didn't help that Toto snapped at my hands when I didn't get it right. I tied her up to a post so I'd have to contend with only the back half of her body and her angry little kicks. My soccer shin guards would have come in handy about then.

I did my best to remember something I'd seen on the Discovery Channel. A show about people living like pioneers. They explained how to milk a cow. I figured it probably had to work the same way with a goat.

After a few minutes, I managed to duplicate what the pioneers had done. I squeezed with my thumb and forefinger and continued squeezing each finger around and down, forcing the milk out in a stream. I kept at it until the milk dried to a dribble and my hands cramped. A quarter of a bucket, maybe four cups. I wondered if it was enough. I set it to the side.

Then I selected a long knife-like tool with sharp, jagged teeth along one edge. I hoped it was a saw, because that's how I planned to use it. A bin near the door overflowed with rags, and I sorted through the collection, pulling out the cleanest bits.

I chopped each branch and trimmed back the V-shaped tops, leaving the whole piece about four feet long. I wrapped strips of cloth around the outside of the V, making a pocket. Into the crook, I stuffed wads of raw wool, then I closed the opening on top. Done! They were crude, but they were crutches, and after trying them out myself, I felt pretty sure that they would help Mark's aunt get around.

∞

I slurped up the last drops of liquid, set the wooden bowl down on the table, and blotted my mouth with my sleeve. Fava bean and onion soup normally wouldn't have been my first choice for dinner, but it was delicious. I picked up my goblet, filled half with wine and half with water, and swigged down a mouthful. Not as bad as I thought it would be.

"Goodness, you must have been hungry." My mother sat on a floor cushion on the opposite side of the table. She rolled a hard-boiled egg back and forth between her palm and the table until the shell crackled into tiny bits.

"That pizza I had at school for lunch today seems like a long time ago." I started to laugh. "You should have seen Tabitha. She had a string of cheese about a yard long between her mouth and her slice . . ." Mom sat immobile across from me. She held the half-peeled egg and just stared at me. My heart skipped a beat as I remembered where I was.

"Pizza? What do you mean?" She stopped, realization spreading across her face. "That was just a dream, Seraphina," she said slowly.

I pulled a plate of goat cheese over to me and cut off a cube. "Was it?" I tossed the cheese into my mouth.

"Of course it was."

"It seems so real, though. I remember everything, even little things. Who can do that with their dreams? What if I really did live in the future?"

She slapped her empty hand against the table, making me jump at the suddenness of it. "Stop saying that!" Her lips pressed themselves into a thin line.

"Why? What if it's true?"

"Do you want people to think you are demon-possessed?" She gave up trying to peel the egg and set it on the plate next to the cheese. She had a point there. People with mental problems weren't always treated kindly even two thousand years in the future. These days, they could be banished. Or stoned to death.

"No more talk of this," she instructed. "Understand?"

My tongue froze, and I nodded. In silence I cleared the dishes from the table and cleaned them with the water I had fetched earlier.

Mom sat down in front of a loom hanging from the wall. Small stone weights dangled from the individual vertical strands of yarn, and they clattered as Mom used a shuttle to work horizontal fibers back and forth through the growing length of fabric.

"Mama?" I asked.

Absorbed in her work, she answered me with a "Hmmm?"

"How long have you known Yeshua?" I dried my hands and sat down again at the table.

Her fingers continued to fly as she shuttled the yarn back and forth, over and under the hanging strands. "Most of my life. When he and his parents would come to Jerusalem for the festivals, they would often stay with us — my father and mother and me, that is."

She stopped her weaving, and her face seemed suddenly younger. "He was like a brother to me. I used to look forward to their visits. Miriam was always so kind to me. And after my mother died, well, we grew closer, I guess you could say."

Mary and I are like this, I remembered her saying to me as she crossed her fingers.

"One year at Passover, after my mother had died, Yeshua was missing for three days, and Joseph and Miriam stayed here while they looked for him. I saw what a close bond there was between mother and child. I wanted that, too. She could tell. From that day on, she made me feel as if *she* were my mother." Mom dabbed at the corner of her eye with the back of her hand and then went back to work.

I stretched out my arm along the table and rested my head on it as I watched my mother work. What was it like for Mom to be mother-less as a child and widowed as a young woman? And to lose her only son? Was it any easier for someone in this time and place than it was for people two thousand years from now? My mother's head was bent over her work, and her shoulders slumped with fatigue. My guess would be no. Family was family, and loss was loss. For all people, for all times.

∞

"Seraphina." My mother held an oil lamp that came into focus as I opened my eyes and lifted my head from the table. "You've fallen asleep. It's time for bed."

I got up from the cushion on the floor and groggily followed her to our room. She pulled off my veil and removed my sandals as I sat on the edge of my bed, eyes half closed, swaying with drowsiness. She whipped back the blanket, and I curled into the mat, grateful to be falling into a slumber that could give my mind some rest. She tucked the blanket up to my chin and brushed her lips against my cheek. I felt as if I were three years old. And I didn't mind at all.

CHAPTER NINE

Mark's aunt threw her mouth open in laughter as her nephew demonstrated using the crutches. A comic performance, if ever there was one, with his tall frame hunched over so his armpits could rest in the crook of the crutches while he held his "injured" foot awkwardly off the floor.

"They're too short for you," I said, looking up from where I was inspecting his aunt's sprained ankle, "because I made them for your aunt." I pelted him with a wadded-up strip of cloth and turned back to my work. The swelling was down a bit, and the deep-purple bruise had already started to fade around the edges to a mustard-ugly blotch that meant it was healing. I used some of the extra lengths of fabric I brought from home to re-bandage the foot, immobilizing it once again.

"All done." I helped her up and positioned the crutches under her arms. After a few minutes, she got the hang of using them. "Now you really should stay off your foot again today. Tomorrow, you can be up and about."

"Thank you," she said, hobbling over to me. She pressed her upper arms against the crutches, securing them to her body and freeing her hands to cup my face. The smell of onions wafted from her fingers. "God will bless you for what you have done." She kissed one cheek, then the other.

Mark picked up a large, empty pitcher from the floor next to the door. "I'll bring you some fresh water," he told his aunt, and the two of us took our leave.

Outside the house, Mark laid his hand on my arm. "I thank you, too," he said. "For your kindness." He squeezed my arm gently, then dropped his gaze. "You would make a fine physician."

"Thanks. I've thought about going to medical school someday, but I'm not sure we can afford it now." A quizzical look passed over his face, and I caught myself. I quickly amended my statement. "I mean, if a woman could be a doctor, I would like that. I enjoy helping people."

To shift the focus from me, I asked what kind of work he would like to do — that is, if he didn't have to follow in his father's trade. He shrugged his shoulders.

"You should use your knowledge of languages," I suggested. "How many languages *do* you know?"

He counted on the fingers of his free hand as he ran through them. "Well, there's Hebrew and Aramaic, of course." Of course. The sacred language and the currently spoken one of the Jews. "And Greek, which we all know, thanks to Alexander's conquest here before the Romans came." His upper lip curled. "And now Latin, *because* of the Romans." More pronounced lip-curling. "There's Coptic, a bit of Syriac, and some of the dialects of Persia." He stopped suddenly and dropped the hand he'd been using for counting, having had to start over on it, looking a bit embarrassed by his abilities. He shrugged. "You know that Jerusalem has many visitors who come from far away. I just pick languages up from the people who do business with my father."

"You could be an interpreter. Or a translator of documents," I said.

His face brightened as he nodded, considering it. "Yes, that would be . . ." His voice trailed off as his eyes took on a faraway look. Then he grew serious and shook his head.

"No, that would be the work of a scholar. I am not a scholar. I stock the back room with the goods my father buys from the traders. And I learn from him. This will be my work someday."

He led me away from the house and down the street to a wide public square. At the far end, a man stood in front of a building addressing the crowd, but he was too far away for us to hear. Roman soldiers patrolled the square on foot, their metal helmets and breastplates glinting in the morning sun. A horse obviously belonging to one of them was tethered to a post on the perimeter of the plaza.

"Seraphina, look at him!" Mark was off in a shot to see the animal up close.

"Uh, very nice," I said when I reached him.

"I've seen this one go all-out. He's really fast." He put down the pitcher, stroked the horse's nose, and scratched him along the jaw line. What was it about boys and horsepower? The animal whinnied and shook his head, jangling an intricate bridle studded with brass medallions. Two soldiers looked up from across the square, and one of them put his hand to the hilt of a short sword secured at his waist.

"I think we'd better go," I urged, pulling on Mark's sleeve. Mark tossed a friendly wave to the soldiers, picked up the jug, and yelled something in Latin to the men. They relaxed and smiled, and one of them said something in response.

"What was that about?" I asked.

"I told them I'd trade them this" — he hiked the pitcher to his shoulder — "for the horse. They said, 'Not even if it was filled with the rarest wine or the most expensive nard.'"

"You've got a gift," I said, shaking my head.

He cocked his head at me, eyebrows raised in question.

"You're good with people. And languages. It's a gift, you know."

He shrugged and led me to the well in the center of the square. "I promised my parents I'd get right back to help set up for tonight, so let's fill this up and take it to my aunt." He lowered a bucket into the well and poured the water into his container, right up to the brim.

"Go ahead," I said. "I'd like to see if Yeshua might be in the Temple today."

Mark bit his lip, considering. "You sure you'll be all right?"

"Yes, fine." I had worn an old, gray mantle, and I pulled it up over my head like a hood. I uncuffed my sleeves and let them hang so that my hands were completely covered. "No one will recognize me." He scrunched his nose at me, looking doubtful.

"I won't be long," I said. "If you see my mother, you can tell her that."

Mark hefted the pitcher onto his shoulder, splashing water over the edge, and retraced his steps toward his aunt's home. Before he left the square, two men stopped him, questioning him about something. I recognized them as two of the men who had been standing at the foot of my bed yesterday when Jesus healed me. One was the young guy; the other was the scruffier-looking older one. I was too far away across the square to hear what they were saying to Mark, but Mark listened for a minute, nodded, and beckoned for them to follow him. And off they went, Mark leading the way with the water, droplets jumping from the pitcher and splashing to the ground where they trailed the trio like asterisks on the dusty flagstones.

I wandered across the square to where the crowd had grown considerably larger and the speechmaker more vocal. I slithered my way through the perspiration-soaked people, my nose unfortunately at the level of too many unwashed armpits. The acrid scent of sweat and dirt burned my nose. Didn't these people *ever* bathe?

Finally, I was at the very front of the crowd looking up at a burly man perched on the ledge of a short wall ringing the building.

". . . to rid ourselves of this blight upon our land," he shouted. Murmurs rippled through the crowd along with a few cheers. "This is *our* land, not theirs. We don't need them here. We don't want them here!" That seemed to draw even more approval. "The Roman scum must leave!" The mob roared its agreement. I twisted around to see if I could spot the soldiers in the square, but I couldn't see over the throng.

The man next to me cupped grimy hands around his mouth and yelled, "You tell them, Bar Abbas!"

I spun on him. "Who is that? What did you say his name is?"

"Bar Abbas," the man said, not even looking down at me. "Yeshua Bar Abbas."

The swarm of people jostled me as they waved their arms and punched the air with clenched fists. Stunned, I barely noticed that the square had taken on the air of a mosh pit. *Bar Abbas.* I had heard the name my whole life, but it was always pronounced "Barabbas," the two words run together. I had always thought it was his first name. All this time, I had it wrong.

Then I remembered Mark calling my brother "Steven Bar Samuel," Steven, son of Samuel. This man standing in front of me and inciting the crowd was "Bar Abbas." *Bar* — "son of" — and *Abbas* — like "Abba," — what Jesus called his Father. And this man's first name was also Yeshua. His first name was Jesus, and his last name was "son of the father." He would be the one to be set free instead of Jesus, Son of the Father.

"An insurrectionist," I whispered to myself. That's what the Gospels said of him. I never understood what that meant before. But at that moment, I knew. Troublemaker. With a capital *T.*

My eyes fixed on his face which was contorted in anger, his eyes blazing with hatred, his mouth spewing venomous words along with sprays of saliva.

"They rape our land, our women. What will be next? *Who* will be next?" he screamed. "You?" He pointed to a woman behind me. "You?" He leaned down to the man standing next to me. "Or will it be our children?" He swung his body toward me, until he was just inches away, his eyes drilling into mine. His hot breath washed across my face, and he reeked strongly of spicy food and wine.

His frenzied speech had whipped up the crowd. I could tell that things were going to get out of control — and quickly. I couldn't let that happen. I had to do something, *anything* to put out the flame he was fanning.

"Please," I begged, my voice too soft for him to hear.

"Please stop," I yelled, getting his attention. "There are other ways. Peaceful ways." If I could reason with him, if I could convince him just to go home quietly, then he would never be arrested. Pilate wouldn't have him to offer to the crowd instead of Jesus. If it came to that. Tomorrow.

He laughed at me and straightened up on the ledge where he stood. "Pax Romana?" he shouted. He spit, and the gob landed near my sandals. "*That* kind of peace, we don't want!" The crowd cheered at his words, and he threw back his head and roared something that sounded like a battle cry.

A man in a striped tunic wormed his way through the crowd and stopped next to me. "Stop this, Bar Abbas! Stop this now!" he shouted. "You only make things worse for everyone."

Bar Abbas sneered at him, pulled a knife from the sheath strapped to his waist, and brandished it in the air. "*They* make things worse for everyone." He pointed the knife over the heads of the people in the crowd, to the opposite side of the square, where I had seen the Roman soldiers. The man next to me leapt unto the ledge next to Bar Abbas.

"NO!" All three of us yelled the word at the same time: Bar Abbas, because he didn't want to be challenged; the man in the striped tunic, because he wanted to stop the madness; and me, because I could see the knife in Bar Abbas' hand arching toward the man.

As the man in the striped tunic lunged toward him, Bar Abbas swung the knife to stop his progress. Because Bar Abbas held the knife so high, the blade met flesh just above the man's tunic. I watched the metal sink sickeningly into his throat until only the hilt was visible. The tip must have come out the back of his neck, but I couldn't tell since I squeezed my eyes shut in horror. The crowd shrieked, cheered, screamed all at once. I opened my eyes and swayed as Bar Abbas yanked out the knife, and blood spurted from the wound. The man tumbled off the ledge and landed at my feet, his breath coming in gurgles and hisses and his eyes lolling back in his head.

I could sense commotion in back of me — the Roman soldiers shoving their way through the crowd, I guessed. The air was charged with shouts and jostling. Faster than a serpent's striking tongue, Bar Abbas' hand shot out and grabbed my elbow. My mantle flew off as he hauled me onto the ledge next to him, nearly dislocating my shoulder. He wrapped his arm around me, securing me to his side. With his other hand, he placed the bloody dagger against my neck and pressed its tip under my jaw.

"Stand back," he shouted. From that vantage point, I could spot the two Roman soldiers about halfway through the crowd, pushing and pressing their way toward us. When they saw me in Bar Abbas' clutches, they stopped.

What could I say to get myself out of this? I had failed at trying to stop this lunatic from murdering. And if he did it once, who was to say he wouldn't do it again?

"Let me go," I begged.

He didn't answer; he merely tightened his hold.

"I'm a no one," I said, but I really wanted to tell him that I was Ronni, that I didn't fit into this scene at all, that I belonged to another time far, far in the future. I squirmed, but I couldn't free myself. Bar Abbas laughed like a madman, and the expression on his face matched his demeanor.

"Don't do this!" I tried to sound firm, not scared. "Let me go!"

His eyes bulged. "Why should I release you? It would be better for you if I killed you today than for that Roman filth to do it tomorrow." The knife point pressed harder, and I squealed.

I struggled to regulate my breathing, to calm my voice. "Look, it's not too late to do the right thing. You hate them" — I nodded in the direction of the soldiers — "because of how they treat our people. But don't you know what they'll do to *you* if you hurt me? Nothing's worth dying for!"

Bar Abbas laughed. "Ah, but some things *are* worth dying for. You need to learn that!"

"But if they kill you, they win! Let me go, and I'll plead for you. You didn't *mean* to kill that man — I'll tell them that."

Other soldiers appeared at the back of the crowd, fighting their way through, shouting and shoving people out of their path. Something blurred in my peripheral vision: a large black mass and a swirl of red. Like machine gun fire, hoof beats clattered on the stones, closer and closer, and the dark bulk of a horse streaked toward me from one side. Without halting the animal, the rider scooped me onto the steed and kicked Bar Abbas from the ledge, all in one fluid movement.

I sat side-saddle on the horse, but there wasn't really a saddle to sit on, just a fancy blanket. And I wasn't actually sitting. My upper half leaned against the horse's neck, and with no saddle horn to grip, I clutched handfuls of mane so as to not fall off.

The soldiers had reached the front of the crowd, and my rescuer reined in his horse and rode over to them. "Arrest that man!" he ordered as the soldiers pinned Bar Abbas to the ground.

I recognized that voice. It was Tabby's dad. I looked over my shoulder. His chest was covered by metal armor with a crimson cape gathered at one shoulder. He wore a metal helmet like the other soldiers, but on the top was what looked like a red-bristled whisk broom.

Another mounted soldier galloped up to us and pulled his horse to a halt. "Centurion Longinus!" the man said.

Tabby's dad clenched his right fist and struck his breast with it, a muffled metal clang coming from the armor. "Tribune!"

"Is everything under control?"

"Yes, Tribune," Mr. Long answered. The soldiers hustled Bar Abbas away, and someone covered the dead man's face with my mantle that had landed on the ground next to him. The crowd quickly dispersed, obviously scared that they would be hauled off, too.

"Do you know this girl?" the tribune asked as he gestured to me.

"Yes," Tabby's father answered.

"See her to safety then."

Mr. Long struck his breast again then drove his heels into his horse. The animal reared up, slamming me against the centurion's chest. He held me tightly around the waist, his thick forearm glistening with sweat and rippling with muscles under fair, curly hairs bright with the sun's light. Despite the warmth of the day, I felt cold, and my stomach quivered and sent shakes down my limbs. My chin trembled uncontrollably, and the buildings began to spin around me. Dizziness and nausea washed over me, and darkness crept into my vision from the edges until my eyesight was focused on one pinprick spot on the ground. I slumped forward. Then everything went black.

CHAPTER TEN

When I came to, I was sitting upright on the horse, leaning back against Mr. Long who supported my chin with his hand. He tilted the opening of a wineskin against my lips and poured the liquid into my mouth. I swallowed instinctively and choked. This stuff wasn't diluted with water like the wine I'd had at dinner.

"More," he ordered.

"No, I —" My protests were cut off by another healthy swig of the wine forced down my throat. This time I didn't choke.

"Thank you," I said, dragging the back of my hand across my mouth. "What happened?"

"You fainted."

In addition to wine, my mouth tasted of vomit, and a glance to the ground confirmed that I had puked up the little that had been in my stomach. The dead man's body had been removed, but a large puddle of blackening blood marked the spot where he had died, and my hands shook as I covered my eyes with them.

Mr. Long released his cape from where it was clasped at his shoulder and let the scarlet material billow around in front of me. He tucked the loose end under his thigh, wrapping me like a burrito.

"I will take you to my home where my wife and daughter can tend to you. It is closer than your house."

"You know where I live?" I asked.

I could hear, rather than see, him smile. "Doesn't my daughter spend most of her time there?"

Did she? Why couldn't I remember that?

We rode slowly out of the square and down the streets where life continued on as if nothing had happened. As if a man hadn't died right in front of me not five minutes ago.

Children played, dogs barked, and women bustled inside the open doorways of their homes. And I was moving farther away from the Temple's entrance. Farther away from finding Jesus. But if I couldn't get to him, maybe Tabby's dad could.

"Mr. Long — I mean, Centurion Longinus? You know of the Rabbi Yeshua, don't you?"

"That rebel?" he asked, somewhat disinterestedly.

"He's not, really. He is a very good man. A holy man. And they want to kill him."

"Who?" The soldier in him was now paying attention.

"Some of the Jewish elders."

"How do you know this?"

What could I say? That I've read the Bible? That I've been taught the story of Jesus' life? That the whole world knows that Christ was crucified?

I scrambled for what to tell him, my sweaty hands creasing wads of the cloak in which I was cocooned. "I've heard of plots against his life." That was true, wasn't it? "Can you do anything to stop them?"

"I cannot interfere with the religious practices of your people. It is of no concern to me."

"You don't care if an innocent man dies?"

"Has he not broken the law?" he asked.

I wanted to laugh. "He . . . he *is* the law."

He grunted. "Watch your tongue, girl! Caesar is the law."

I dropped the subject. He wouldn't be able to help. He couldn't. He dug his heels into the horse's side, and the mount reared up a little. I snaked my hands out from under the cloak and laced my fingers into the mane, holding onto the coarse horsehair for dear life.

∞

We stopped in front of a small home along a lane not far from the Antonia Fortress. The centurion swung down from the horse and lifted me easily from the animal's back. Mr. Long was a big man, and standing next to him, my head barely reached his chest. I looked up to thank him, but stopped when I saw him with his fingertips pressed against his eyelids and his square jaw clamped so tightly, veins bulged in his neck.

Tabby's mother rushed from the house. "Cassius, not again!" She pulled off his helmet, revealing sweat-soaked auburn hair plastered to his head. She pried his fingers from his eyes, and I could see the bloodshot whites of them. She led him through the doorway, under which he had to duck, and I followed them to find Tabby inside.

"Will your father be okay?" I asked Tabby as Mrs. Long took her husband into a back room.

Tabby fluttered her hand as if to dismiss it. "He'll be fine. This happens all the time." But her eyes kept darting to the other room where her parents spoke in hushed tones. Then she drew her breath in sharply. "What happened to you?"

"What?"

She grabbed a cloth from the table, dipped it into a basin of water, and pressed it against my neck just under my jaw. When she pulled it away, it was bloodstained. I hadn't even realized Bar Abbas had cut me.

"Oh, that." I filled her in on what had just happened. The only good part of reliving the horrid experience was that it distracted Tabby from what was wrong with her dad.

I took the cloth from her, blotted at the knife prick, and handed it back to her. "Thanks." I removed her father's cloak, folded it on the table, and rose to leave.

"Where are you going?" she asked.

"I've got to get back. I'm late already."

"Ah, yes. Passover."

"You know of it?" I asked.

"Mark invited me to join his family at the meal. Even though Jews are not supposed to dine with Gentiles. He said it would be all right, though, for even Yeshua eats with Gentiles."

An ache sprang up in the pit of my stomach, and I fought down the jealousy.

"Yes," I admitted. "He does."

"My father won't let me go, though," Tabby continued.

Good, I thought, and then felt ashamed. Tabby was my friend, after all. She had risked her life for me. I should be happy for her that Mark liked her. *Should* be.

"I'll walk part of the way with you," she volunteered as she pulled her shawl over her cornflower-blue gown. She handed me my burgundy mantle from yesterday, and I flipped it over my shoulder as we walked out into the bright sunshine.

"Don't you get lonely here in Jerusalem?" I asked. "So far from home?"

"It's all right," she said. "When my father was first assigned here, he was gone for a whole year. We really missed him. That's when my mother insisted we move here. Even though father lives in the barracks of the fortress, we still get to see him. And now, with his eyes as they are . . . well, I'm glad we're here. But I do miss our home."

"You'll go back to Rome someday," I said.

She shook her head. "We won't go back there. If my father's eyes get worse . . ." She paused and gathered her cloak around her before she continued.

"My father comes from a wealthy family, and they want us to live with them in Neapolis. Actually, down the coast a bit. It's beautiful there."

Neapolis? Did she mean Naples?

"We'll have the sea at our doorstep and pools fed by hot springs. And the beautiful mountain against our backs. It is sunny and green. A wonderful place to live."

I drew up short and turned to face her. "You don't mean Pompeii, do you?"

"No. Why?"

I let out my breath in a rush, not even aware that I'd been holding it. "Oh, good. I thought maybe your grandparents lived there and the mountain was Vesuvius."

"It is," she said. "But my grandparents' home is along the coast, in Herculaneum."

Adrenalin shot through me from my temples to my toes. Not Herculaneum! Like Pompeii, it would be doomed when Vesuvius erupted. In history class, I had never been good about memorizing all those dates, but that was one of only a handful that had stuck in my head: 1776, America becomes a country; 1620, pilgrims land at Plymouth Rock; 1492, Columbus discovers the New World; 1436, Gutenberg invents the printing press; 1095, the Crusades start; 312 A.D., Constantine converts to Christianity; 79 A.D., Vesuvius erupts.

"What is it?" Tabby's eyes were huge and her face as white as mine must have been. How could I tell her this? How could I explain what would happen in the future?

"Tabitha," I began tentatively. "You know how when I was sick, I dreamed that I lived in the future? Way in the future?"

She tried to look as if she didn't know what I was talking about.

"I know Mark told you," I said.

"All right. So what?"

"There were a lot of things that I learned that had happened in the past. I mean, the past that had happened before the point in time where I was living. Does that make sense?"

"Not really," she said.

"Look, if I was living a thousand years from now, and somebody picked me up and plopped me here in this time, I'd know everything that happened in the thousand years between now and then. Follow me?"

"I think so . . ." I could see her turning over in her mind what I had said. Then the expression on her face morphed from one of confusion to one of alarm.

"What's going to happen?" she asked, grasping the fact that I knew something about *her* future.

"I don't know. I mean, I don't know if it *will* happen. How could it? I can't have lived in the future, can I?" It was a question that neither of us could answer. "Just promise me one thing."

"What?"

"Promise me that you won't be living anywhere near Vesuvius from the time you're . . ." How old would she be? I stopped to do the calculation. If this was 33 A.D., that meant that Vesuvius would blow in forty-six years. Tabby would be fifty-nine then. Or sixty, depending on when during the year it happened. But I knew that the exact year of Jesus' birth was debated, so the current year probably wasn't really 33. To be on the safe side, I knocked off nine years. "Don't be anywhere near that mountain from the time you are fifty years old."

She smiled. Fifty years old seemed like an eternity away, even to me.

"I mean it, Tabitha. Promise me. You won't come within a hundred miles of the area. Promise me!" I hadn't realized that my hands were on her biceps until I'd given her a stern shake. Her face grew solemn.

"But, why?" she asked rubbing the spots on her arms that I had gripped.

"Just promise!"

"All right, I promise," she said, her voice barely a whisper.

"Good." I had seen those pictures in my history book of the molds made of the bodies that were incinerated in Vesuvius' ashes. People screaming. Families clinging together. Lives stopped in mid-motion. Would Tabby remember my warning? Would she become one of those caught in the volcano's fury? An acid taste burned in the back of my throat, and no matter how often I swallowed, it wouldn't go away.

CHAPTER ELEVEN

My mother hustled around the kitchen, placing things into a basket to take to the Passover meal. "Fire," she muttered. "We'll need to start one for cooking . . ." With tongs, she plucked a glowing coal from the banked fire and deposited it into a small, lidded piece of crockery pierced with holes.

"Carry this, please," she said, wrapping the warm bowl in a cloth and handing it to me. Great. Didn't she know how bad I was with fire, I thought, remembering the torch burning out in the tunnel. A young Prometheus I was not.

"Wear your good cloak," she instructed. I set down the warm bowl to slip my arms into the linen garment.

"And your veil!" she added as I moved toward the door bare-headed. I deftly whipped the tea towel over my hair and secured it behind my neck. I was getting good at that.

I followed her out of the house and up the hill behind our modest dwelling. Long, wide terraces stepped their way higher, flanked by pink-flowering rockrose bushes and thorny broom plants thick with yellow blossoms. Honeysuckle vines crept through the shrubs, releasing an intoxicating scent that hooked itself into my nostrils and pulled me along the path. I felt drugged, like Dorothy tripping through the poppy field.

A set of outside stairs climbed to the second floor of a building. Mom led the way, and I followed her up the stairs and through the open door. Crossing the threshold, I stopped at what I saw, frozen to the spot, my mouth hanging wide open. I wouldn't have been more surprised to have seen the Wicked Witch of the West standing there.

It was Maggie. The girl my mom had brought to youth group in . . . my other life. Maggie, who was so boy-crazy. The one I always thought of as a skank. Here she stood. Clean-scrubbed, completely covered-up Maggie. Beautiful Maggie. My mother embraced her as best she could with full arms, and Maggie returned the hug, then relieved Mom of her burdens.

Maggie tossed me a genuine smile before she hurried to the other side of the room where food was being prepared.

Mark appeared at my side. "What is it?" he asked. "You look like you've seen a ghost."

"Mag—" I just pointed at her.

"Oh, Mary. Of Magdala. Didn't you expect her? She has been one of the master's most devoted disciples. I would have been surprised if she *hadn't* been here tonight."

My attention was diverted then by Mark's parents, who greeted me and my mother. I wondered if they owned this upper room, which appeared to be used solely for entertaining. Mark's mom took the coal from me and used it to get a fire burning in what looked like a large fireplace.

"Mark!" his mother called, but he apparently didn't hear.

"John Mark!" she repeated, more insistently. His ears perked up then. Apparently, even in the first century, when mothers really wanted you to do something, they used both your first *and* middle names. He hurried over to her at the fire.

My eyes scanned the huge room where evenly placed pillars supported an intricate barrel-vaulted ceiling. Torches and lanterns were affixed to the walls and the columns, and Mark took a twist of straw from his mother, lit it in the fireplace, and went to work lighting up the room. I closed my eyes and inhaled. The room smelled exactly like the inside of St. Augustine's Church right after the altar servers extinguished the sanctuary candles — that smoky, waxy odor that calms the soul and invites silence, prayer, and reflection.

When was the last time I'd taken advantage of that and prayed, really prayed? It didn't take long for me to answer that question. I stopped praying the day of the funeral for Dad and Steven. When I begged God to bring them back. When he said, "No."

I opened my eyes and caught Mark staring at me before he quickly turned away. I must have looked like a super-goof standing there, eyes shut, breathing deeply. No wonder he had asked Tabby to come to the dinner. That way he wouldn't have been stuck with me. Too bad for him that she had said no.

Mom set me to work chopping some green leaves she called *eryngo*. They looked exactly like the dandelion weeds I yanked from our yard each summer, and when I sampled one, I discovered they tasted about that awful, too. Maggie and my mother sat on the floor digging almonds out of their shells, two large bowls between them — one for the nuts, the other for the shells.

"Could you use some help?" A middle-aged man sat down next to them, joined by a woman who must have been his wife.

"Say yes, before he changes his mind," the woman said. "Back home, I can never get him to help prepare a meal."

"Cleopas! Mary! Yes, thank you!" My mother handed them each a large scoop of nuts and two small hammers. "You crack, we'll remove."

Mary gently slapped her husband's hand as he reached for the shelled nuts. "No eating. These are for the meal."

"Do you suppose there might be some left over?" Cleopas whispered, his eyes twinkling. "I sure would like a few for that walk back to Emmaus."

"I think we can arrange that," my mother answered. "When will you be leaving?"

"On the morning after the Sabbath," Mary said.

Cleopas said something that sent them all into fits of laughter, but I couldn't hear, thanks to the squeals of a herd of children running past me.

Men hauled low dining tables into the room, setting them up along the perimeter, and the children ran back and forth, placing cushions and mats on the floor around the tables. Two of the men I recognized as the guys who had stopped Mark in the square earlier in the day. They helped position a very large table in the center of the room.

The place hummed with the activity of meal preparation, and I, being the closest to the door, was the only one who heard the knock. I pressed my eye to a crack between two weather-beaten boards in the door. All I could see were colorful robes, finely made. And very long tassels. The garb of a Pharisee — just like the clothes of the man who wanted me arrested because of my eczema. I turned my back against the wood.

"Is someone there, Seraphina?" my mother asked, coming across the room.

I nodded, and when she got close enough, I whispered, "It's a Pharisee." Those close enough to hear stopped their chattering, and the silence swept across the room.

"Well, let's open the door," Mom said, and she did. "Joseph! Oh, Joseph, please come in!" She reached through the entranceway and drew an older man into the room. He had the look of Santa Claus about him — long silver hair poking out of his head covering and melting into a matching beard flowing onto his chest. Red circles punctuated his cheeks, and his eyes swam with a dark, watery color I couldn't quite pinpoint.

"For the master's table," he said. He stretched out his arms, offering up a length of fine, cream-colored fabric woven in a herringbone pattern.

My mother took it from him. "A tablecloth. It's gorgeous. Thank you so much." She handed me the material and embraced Joseph, embarrassing him a bit, I could tell by his reaction. "Please, stay and have your Passover meal here. I know it is your custom to dine with other Pharisees, but we would welcome your company tonight."

He looked kindly at my mother. "No, Salome, I cannot, but I thank you." He bowed slightly and backed out of the door.

My mother picked up two corners of the tablecloth, and I grabbed the other two. We snapped it between us, and the fabric billowed upward like a parachute and gently floated down. At a length of more than twelve feet and a width about a quarter of that, it covered the long center table like a runner.

"It's beautiful," I said, smoothing the bubbles in the tablecloth. "Who was that man?"

"Joseph? He's a Pharisee. A good, holy man. Born in Arimathea, but he has lived in Jerusalem for many, many years."

Joseph of Arimathea? I had to catch him. "I'll be right back," I said as I rushed to the door.

Outside, I sprinted down the staircase and followed the terraced path away from the upper room. In the distance I could see Joseph walking with a slight shuffle to his gait. I hurried up to him and slowed my pace to match his.

He startled slightly at my appearance, a questioning look in his eyes. I remembered what had happened when I spoke to the Pharisee in the Temple. Was I crazy to try to talk to another Pharisee here? There was only one way to find out, and what I had to say was too important for me to keep silent.

I cleared my throat. "I just wanted to thank you again," I said. "And ask a favor." I held my breath, waiting to see how he would respond.

His face softened, and he inclined an ear toward me. "You are welcome. And what, my child, might that favor be?"

"I know you are a faithful man. You believe Yeshua is the Christ." His eyes shifted back and forth in an attempt to ascertain who might have heard what I just said. "But fear stops you," I added more quietly. "Us. Fear stops all of us." He lowered his eyes in an admission of guilt. "But I can guarantee, your devotion to the Lord will play itself out. Soon."

His thin lips spread into a feeble smile. "Am I to believe that you, child, are a prophetess? Another Deborah or Huldah?"

"Maybe I am," I said simply. "Or maybe not. But I think you know something as well as I do."

"Know what?"

"That the scribes and the Pharisees —" I stopped for a second. "I mean, some of the Pharisees, are plotting to kill Yeshua." The smile that lingered on his lips evaporated like steam from a kettle. "You've got to promise me that you will try to stop them."

He shrugged and lifted his palms. "What can I do? I am just one man."

"So was David. And he defeated the whole Philistine army."

He patted my arm. "I am no David."

"No," I said. "You are Joseph of Arimathea. Disciple of Yeshua, the Christ."

He was quiet for a long time, considering. "The sentiment against him is so strong," he said. "I am not sure I can have any effect. But I will do what I can." He patted my arm again.

"That's all I ask. Thank you." I stood on my tiptoes and pecked him on the cheek. He hobbled away, carrying my hopes on his narrow shoulders.

I'd been gone longer than I intended, and I ran back to the Passover dinner. With puffing breaths, I rushed up the stairs to the upper room, my heart drumming under my breastbone. I had hope, real hope that Joseph could do something to sway the Pharisees.

I opened the door, slipped in quietly, and froze. They were all there. While I'd been gone, the men had arrived, and they had arranged themselves around the table. The picture of them looked like it could be a painting, but one thought struck me with the force of an ax blow: da Vinci got it wrong.

CHAPTER TWELVE

The men weren't sitting in chairs all along one side of a single table with Jesus smack in the center as Leonardo had painted the scene. Two shorter tables butted up to the main table, perpendicular to it at each end. The arrangement of tables formed a stretched-out *U.* The men lounged on floor mats around the low table with Jesus, as host, occupying the center of the short section making up the left wing.

My eyes locked on him, and I think I surely must have stopped breathing. Even though I had seen Jesus yesterday, I hadn't known then who he was. But to be here now, with the full understanding that I was seeing him right before me — it was almost more than I could get my mind around. He was real. Human. Here. With me. I stood paralyzed.

There was nothing about him that marked him as extraordinary, and yet he was the center of attention. A warm smile spread across his face and sparked in his ebony eyes. He had a short mustache and beard with thick black hair that brushed his shoulders. A high forehead, wide-set eyes, and a strong nose didn't make him look different from any of the other men. He could have been taken for anyone's husband, father, brother, teacher, or friend, but something set him apart as the most attractive person in the room — perhaps it was his eyes, which seemed as if they missed nothing at all.

He looked up at me, as if he knew I watched him, and he smiled, laugh lines crinkling around his eyes. A surge of electricity shot through me. I pulled my eyes from his face, embarrassed that I had been staring, not having the courage to approach or speak to him. From the corner of my eye, I saw him turn back to his friends, and I directed my interest to the men scattered around the table.

To his right, on the end, was "Zeke," the younger of the two brothers who had been standing by my bedside yesterday morning, and one of the men I had seen talking to Mark in the square earlier in the day. That had to be John.

On the other side of Jesus, in what was the place of honor, sat a man with a quiet, cheerless expression who kept his eyes fastened to the table. Across from them, along the other short side of the table, I recognized "Hunk," the other brother. That would be James. And next to him, "Hickory," the other man in the square that morning, and at my bedside yesterday. The husky one with wild hair and scraggly beard: Peter.

I glanced around the table at each apostle's face in turn. There was nothing remarkable about any of them — in looks or in manner. They were ordinary men. Destined to live extraordinary lives.

The women brought serving dishes to the table — pottery bowls of shelled nuts, platters of peeled hard-boiled eggs, and dishes containing various sauces and the bitter herbs I'd chopped earlier. One of them brought in a basket of warm flat bread that looked like pita, and its freshly baked smell made my mouth water. She set it on a table off to the side. My mother, Mark's mother, Mary Magdalen, and Cleopas' wife, Mary, shuttled back and forth from the food preparation tables and the fire to the long main table and the smaller ones off to the side where other people sat.

And Miriam was there, too. She placed several branches of cut rockroses into a clay vase and tenderly set it on the floor in front of the low, horseshoe-shaped dining table. The flowers were lovely, but their aroma was hard to catch. When the scent did hit me, I grinned, relishing the delicacy of the fragrance. I noticed Miriam inhaling deeply, too, and when I caught her eye, she smiled. We paused but a moment, sharing the beauty of the roses before she continued her work, pouring wine into goblets and gently resting a hand on her son's shoulder as she passed behind him.

She set the empty wine pitcher on a little table, and I approached her slowly. She turned in my direction.

"Blessed Mother," I said, lifting her hands to my lips. "Thank you for being there yesterday with Yeshua. In my room." She smiled and drew me close to her.

"Yeshua," I began, not knowing exactly how to finish what I wanted to say. I glanced over at him sitting at the table. Then I looked back to his mother. "He cured me," I whispered, as if she didn't already know that. She smiled even more brightly. "And I'm so grateful for that. But my brother and my father . . ." I placed my hand against my heart where that sorrow still ached. "It hurts, and I can't make it stop."

She used an edge of her veil to dab at my leaky eyes, then she gently turned me toward Jesus, and with her mouth against my ear said, "Do whatever he tells you." She put her hand on my back with just enough pressure to start me walking in his direction.

Jesus stood from the table and met me halfway. I sank to my knees in front of him, but he lifted me gently by the hands and guided me to a bench against the wall. I clung to his fingers, certain that I was going to slip away from him or that he was going to evaporate from my grasp. I swallowed hard, but not a drop of saliva was forced down my throat.

"Lord," I croaked. I cleared my throat and started over. "I didn't want you to think I was like the nine lepers. I want to thank you. For making me well." He squeezed my hands as the corners of his lips turned up.

The pain in my chest still felt very real. "But my brother. My father — I miss them so much."

He cupped my chin in his hand. "Greater love has no man than this: that a man lay down his life for his friends."

"But it wasn't a friend. They died saving a . . . saving a stranger!" There, it was out.

"Ah," he said. "One of the least of my brethren." He folded me into his arms.

Shame flooded my face and burned the tips of my ears. "Forgive me," I cried into his chest. "It just hurts knowing that they are gone forever."

He placed his hands on my shoulders, forcing me to look at him. "Truly, truly, I say to you, he who hears my word and believes him who sent me, has eternal life; he does not come into judgment, but has passed from death to life."

I thought about what he said. Eternal life for those who believed in him. I know Steven believed in Jesus, but Dad? "My brother, yes," I said, "but my father?" He never went to church with us. I don't think he ever read the Bible. "He didn't know you!"

Jesus raised his eyebrows at that, challenging me on the truth of that statement.

"He *didn't* know you, did he?" I asked. His nod was ever so slight.

"Let not your heart be troubled," he said. "Believe in God; believe also in me. In my Father's house are many rooms." He kissed my cheek with the softness of a spring morning, and then he stood and returned to the table.

I rested my hand against the side of my face. I still missed Dad and Steven horribly, but Jesus had given me hope. It was a conversation I should have had with him months ago. And it made me even more determined to stop the crucifixion.

My mother motioned to me to help her, and when I reached her side, she placed in my arms a platter of the still-warm flatbread. With a gentle push, she propelled me toward the main table.

I am an altar server, I thought, as I put one foot carefully in front of the other, crossed behind John, and walked toward Jesus, suddenly realizing what was going to happen. He sat up from where he had been reclining and gently tugged on my sleeve so that I knelt next to him with the platter in my arms. He took the bread and set it on the table, and I started to get up to leave, but he placed his hand on my arm, indicating that he wanted me to stay. Then with both hands he elevated one of the circles of bread and prayed a blessing.

"Take and eat," he said. "This is my body, which will be given for you. Do this in memory of me." He broke off a piece and handed it to John. A larger piece he passed to his left for the others to share, but a small portion remained in his hand. He turned to me and held it up between his thumb and first two fingers, offering it to me.

Tears flooded my eyes, blurring the scene in front of me. The brown morsel he held blended with his hand; I couldn't tell where his fingers ended and the fragment began. It was all the same.

The Body of Christ. No one said the words, but they sounded in my head. I cupped my hands and whispered, "Amen." He laid it on my palm, and I picked it up and placed it in my mouth. My right hand automatically went to my forehead to bless myself, but then I stopped. People didn't use the Sign of the Cross here . . . yet.

I turned the gesture into a scratch, and a soft smile tugged at his lips. He raised his right hand, the first two fingers pointing upward, the thumb and the others curved toward his palm. He was blessing me. I had received the first Eucharist and was on my knees in front of him whose body I was consuming. I stood and quietly backed away from the table.

Jesus picked up the full goblet in front of him and raised it as far up as his arms extended, his sleeves sliding down to his elbows and revealing the long muscles of his forearms, taut and straight.

"This cup is the new covenant in my blood, which will be shed for you," he said, his voice strong and determined. "Drink from it, all of you."

A hush settled over the room as the cup passed from one man to another and each drank. The last man put down the cup, and everyone sat unmoving, as if frozen in time, but after a few moments, activity resumed, and the men continued to eat and quietly converse.

Shortly thereafter, an expression of sorrow clouded Jesus' face. "Amen, I say to you, one of you will betray me."

Stunned silence filled the room — hands paused over dishes and mouths stopped in mid-chew as the apostles looked from one to another.

"Surely it is not I, Lord?" one of the men asked.

"Nor I?" said another.

"Not me."

"I would never —"

"No!"

From the opposite side of the table, Peter caught John's eye. With a slight jerk of his head and a wrinkle of his brow, the older man conveyed to the younger that he was to ask Jesus who the betrayer was.

John leaned back, rested his head against Jesus' chest and asked, "Master, who is it?"

Jesus picked up a piece of food before answering. "It is the one to whom I hand the morsel after I have dipped it." He tapped the bit of food into one the shallow bowls holding a sauce, then offered it to the man on his left.

Judas paused for a moment, his face full of uncertainty as he looked at the piece of food, then he raised his eyes to Jesus' face and let them travel back down to the morsel. Slowly, he reached out, and his fingers closed around the food, brushing Jesus' hand as he took the morsel from him.

Judas' face hardened then, a dark shadow passing over his features, hollowing his eyes and accentuating the vertical creases running alongside his down-turned mouth. The other apostles watched with curious expressions on their faces, as if they didn't understand what was going on.

Jesus squared his shoulders and spoke directly to Judas. "What you are going to do, do quickly." Judas rose so rapidly that his knee struck the edge of the table, causing the earthenware serving dishes to clink against each other and wine to slosh to the edges of goblets. As swiftly as a sudden breeze kicks up, he blew past me, his robes swishing with each long stride. At the door he paused and turned back to look at Jesus, his face chiseled as if in rock. Then he was gone.

I immediately ran to the door. Mark intercepted me. "Where are you going?" he asked.

"To stop him!"

"From what? He's probably going to buy something for the feast. Or to give money to the poor."

"He's not! He's going to turn Yeshua over to the elders," I said in a frantic whisper, trying to sidestep Mark.

He blocked me easily. "What makes you think that?"

"Didn't you hear?" My voice was louder than I intended, and several people glanced our way. I lowered it again. "Don't any of you ever really listen to what Yeshua says to you?"

As I heard my own question, I slapped my hand against my mouth. Who was I to criticize them? I had two thousand years of perspective on the words of Jesus, and did I heed them?

"I'm sorry," I murmured. "But Judas will betray him. Tonight."

Mark placed his hands on my elbows. "Seraphina, really —"

I tried to pull my arms from his grip. "I know you don't believe me, but I have to do this." I looked back to the table where Jesus sat with his head slightly bowed. "I owe Yeshua everything. He gave me back my life. It must have been for some purpose. This is it. Something awful is going to happen unless I stop it."

Someone in the room began singing, "O give thanks to the LORD, for he is good; his steadfast love endures forever!" Soon, everyone joined in the hymn, and the room was filled with a choir of voices.

Mark drilled me with a stern look. "Don't do this," he said.

"I must."

"You're just a foolish little girl!"

With a tremendous wrench, I pulled my arms out of his hands, and not bothering with my cloak, I rushed out the door into the black night, the verse of the psalm trailing after me as I ran down the steps two at a time. On a hunch, I abandoned the terraced pathway leading downward and raced along a narrow lane winding in the other direction. Mark had delayed me so long, I wasn't certain I could catch Judas, and I wouldn't have, except I could see he had paused up ahead, his back pressed against a wall, his face buried in his hands.

I stopped short in front of him. "You don't have to do this," I said. He hadn't heard me approach, and his face snapped up from his hands, his eyes filled with surprise, his cheeks moist with tears. I laid my hands on his arms. He didn't resist.

"Whatever your reasons, whatever good you think you are doing, please reconsider." I said. He dropped his head and shook it, a mournful groan rising out of him.

"If you don't stop, this isn't going to end well," I said. "For Yeshua or you." He nodded, and I thought perhaps I had convinced him, but then a wail surged from within him, stronger and stronger, sounding as if it was coming from the depths of his soul, from the very recesses of his heart. He shook my hands off him and rushed away from me, his dark cloak melting with the blackness of the night which folded around him and seemed to drag him down, down into nothingness.

When I got back to the upper room, Jesus and the apostles were gone. The women were busy with their work, clearing dishes and wiping tables. Jesus' mother leaned forward, sweeping crumbs from the table into her hand. Her face looked pinched with worry, and then her veil swung forward, blocking her profile from my view. She couldn't possibly know what was happening now, could she? She wasn't God. But she *was* a mother.

I pulled my cloak from the peg and slipped it on. Mark grabbed my arm. "Now what?" he demanded.

"I must find Yeshua," I said, uncurling his fingers from my arm.

"But they've gone off to pray."

"On the Mount of Olives, right?" I spun to face Mark. "He'll be arrested there. Mark, he's in danger!"

He appeared struck by my words. "But the people love him."

"They will turn on him. Soon. He will be crucified."

Mark's face contorted in horror. "But crucifixion is for criminals. Yeshua isn't a criminal!"

"You're right. But it will happen unless I can stop it."

"Seraphina, please. I believe you *think* you know what's going to happen. I believe you *think* you lived in the future . . ."

"No, Mark, I *do* know what's going to happen. Whether I lived in the future, or just had a dream, or was given a vision, I can't say. All I know is that something awful is going to happen. I know it. I have to stop it. And I could use your help."

He stood staring at me, completely silent. My rage boiled up inside me. "If you won't come with me, I'll go alone."

"But, Sera—"

I shot him an angry look, yanked open the door, and rushed out into the cool evening air, flipping the hooded portion of the cloak up onto my head.

I paused at the bottom of the stairs. The men were nowhere in sight. But I didn't need to see them to know where they were going. The Mount of Olives lay outside the wall of the city, directly east of the Temple. I remembered Mr. Josephson telling us that Jesus stood on the mount looking west toward the Temple when he had predicted its destruction.

I thought the street would be difficult to follow in the dark, but the moon was bright. And nestled between the large, flat stones that paved the roadway, I saw something interesting. Small, diamond-shaped reflective rocks separated the larger stones on the road. They shone with an iridescence all their own. Natural nightlights. They made it simple to pick out the road. What a concept! Why weren't these rocks along the edges of every road in America? Maybe that would help keep drunk drivers from running off the road. Then nobody would have to stop to help them. And risk their lives.

I pushed those thoughts from my mind and began running northward. When I reached the Temple, I broke to my right and fled through the gate and down out of Jerusalem toward the ridge rising east of the city. Heading into the dark night. Toward the turning point in history. Toward the cruelty of its reality. Toward the uncertainty of whether I could alter the future.

CHAPTER THIRTEEN

I picked my way down toward the valley. There wasn't another person in sight — a fact that both relieved and terrified me. While I was glad that no one would stop me, I wasn't all that thrilled about being out after dark by myself. It was something my mother didn't let me do in the twenty-first century. I doubt she'd like it now.

A creature howled in the distance, and I froze in place. "The Lord is my light and my salvation; whom should I fear?" I repeated the line from the psalm over and over until my feet agreed to start moving again.

The path continued to curve eastward, but I had no real sense of where I was going. I stopped to listen, to see if I could hear something — singing, praying, anything that might point me in the right direction. No voices reached me through the night air, only the sound of chirping crickets in the tall grass up ahead. I scanned the hill for torch light, but saw only black masses that could have been bushes or boulders . . . or bodies.

A hand latched onto my shoulder, and I let loose with a blood-curdling scream.

"Seraphina, it's me," Mark panted as he twirled me around to face him. I could barely hear him with the blood pounding away like a huge bass drum in my ears. Sweat beaded on his brow. "I thought you'd come back, but when you didn't . . ." He bent over, hands on knees, and drew in huge gulps of air. "I didn't think I could catch you."

He must have waited a long time before he made his decision to follow me, and then did so hurriedly, because he hadn't bothered to grab a cloak. Or maybe he thought he'd talk me into coming back right away. Well, he was wrong.

"I'm not going back," I said.

"All right." His dark brows hooded his deep-set eyes, but I could see him trying to make a decision. "Then I'll go with you."

Yes! Score one point for me!

"They'll be at Gethsemane," I said. "Do you know where that is?"

"I do."

∞

We tramped our way across the valley in the darkness, thankful for the light of a full moon, which was diminished only slightly when wispy clouds floated across it. We stopped at the bank of a shallow creek too wide to jump. Mark searched for a place where exposed rocks hopscotched their way across the water. He took the lead, gingerly stepping from one stone to another as I clung to his hand and put my foot where his had just been.

At the far bank, moss covered the rocks over which the stream skimmed ever so slightly. "It will be slick here," he said. He grabbed me by my forearms and swung me from the dry rock on which I was standing to the squishy moistness of the bank. I was safe, but he wasn't.

Mark's feet shuffled back and forth on the slippery rocks, picking up speed as he tried to maintain his balance. In the end the rocks won, and with his arms whirling like propellers, Mark tumbled backwards and splashed into the water, yelling a word I'd never heard before, but what I could only assume was a first-century curse word.

I smothered a laugh as Mark scrambled out of the stream as quickly as possible.

"C-c-cold," he stammered.

"The water?" I asked.

He glared at me. "Yes. The water. The air. Me." He flicked his arms, sending droplets toward me, and he shook his head like a wet dog. His hair rose up in curls, the longer lengths forming wide, dripping ringlets that stuck to his neck. Beads of water clung to his long eyelashes, and in the moonlight, they glistened like stars. His wet tunic was fused to his chest, showing off a tight six-pack and broad shoulders. But I didn't let myself stand gawking in admiration since his teeth were chattering and goosebumps were rising on his forearms.

"Here," I said, peeling off my cloak. "Wear this."

"No."

"Come on, you gave me yours yesterday. Besides, you can't stay in those wet clothes. You'll catch your death of pneumonia." Man, I sounded like my mother.

Mark wrinkled his brow. "Newmoan . . . what?"

I chuckled to myself. I knew a word he didn't, but I bet he could figure it out — surely it came from Latin or Greek. "Never mind," I said. "Catch up to me after you change." I tossed my cloak onto a scrub oak and then merged with the darkness down the path.

∽

"This doesn't fit at all." Mark's wet clothes were spread on a bush to dry, and he stood next to me wearing my cloak which hit him just above the knees and pulled tightly across his back while the sleeves extended only a few inches beyond his elbows. For modesty's sake, he clutched the front together with both hands, one high and one low, to ward off an embarrassing moment.

"Sorry. It will have to do," I said. The seriousness of my mission hit me suddenly. The lightness of what had just happened dissolved, and I hurried down the path. "We don't have much time."

The full moon lighted our way into the olive grove where leafy branches extended from thick ancient trunks twisted like old men bent over on their canes. Bumps and knobs on the contorted bark transformed the wood into dozens and dozens of faces staring at us, reminding me of the talking apple trees in the enchanted forest in *The Wizard of Oz*.

A feeling that we shouldn't be there washed over me with a shiver. The moonlight filtered through the trees' silver-green leaves, casting eerie shadows on the ground. I thought for a moment that soon we were going to get pelted by fruit. Luckily for us, it wasn't olive season.

An owl hooted somewhere in the distance, and I tucked myself behind Mark, grasping his arm with both hands.

The thicket finally gave way to an open space, and at last I could draw in a complete breath. The scent of spring hung like a net over the garden. An odor of sweet blossoms floated on the air, a distinct smell I couldn't quite identify, but one that drummed up memories of hard candy, a scented bath, or freshly squeezed juice.

Skinny cypress trees stood like sentinels, tall dark soldiers posted to guard an olive press. The stone base of the press was circular, about six feet in diameter, with a lip encircling the rim. A large stone wheel with a hollowed-out core sat on its edge just inside the rim, and through the hole was a long wooden pole used to roll the wheel around the inside of the base. So this was how olive oil was made — by sheer crushing force.

I ran my hand along the inside lip of the empty press. A thin coat of oil from last year's pressing shone on my fingertips. Turning my back on Mark, I secretly anointed myself, touching the oil in a Sign of the Cross on my chest where my gown opened at the neck. A blessing. A prayer that I could do what I was supposed to do.

I turned back to see Mark up ahead gesturing to me. When I reached him, he pulled me down next to him behind a large bush.

"Mark, what —"

"Shhh." He pointed through an opening framed by two cypresses. Jesus was on his knees, face turned heavenward, moonlight illuminating his features. He threw himself against a huge, flat boulder, his arms embracing it and his shoulders shaking with grief for several minutes.

"Abba, Father," his voice came to us, strong and pleading, "all things are possible to you. Take this cup away from me, but not what I will, but what you will." He dropped his face into his hands, and I turned away, my eyes searching for the apostles.

Three of them were huddled together at the base of a tree, obviously deeply asleep. Farther down the slope, the remaining men had stretched out on the ground, also soundly sleeping.

Jesus stood up and walked between the two groups of men. "Are you still sleeping and taking your rest?" he asked loudly. The men began to stir. "It is enough. The hour has come. Behold, the Son of Man is to be handed over to sinners."

The apostles roused themselves, yawning, stretching, and looking sheepishly at the Lord. Jesus held each one's gaze in turn, and the look on his face explained it all to me. He didn't need them to be awake and present for *his* sake only; it was also for *their* sake. How often in the past three years had he warned them to watch because they didn't know the hour or the day? And now this was the hour. His hour. And they'd been sleeping. They'd thrown the chance away.

The men were fixed in place as if immortalized in a religious painting. Time stopped, but for just a moment. Then Judas emerged from the darkness, and behind him, pinpricks of light bobbed through the trees as dozens of guards carried their torches aloft. The small clearing was immediately filled with men brandishing weapons. A whole army for one man. I tried to get up, but Mark wouldn't let me.

Judas stopped in front of Jesus. "Rabbi," he said, and grasping Jesus by the shoulders, he leaned in to kiss him on the cheek. Judas' face caught the moonlight, and in that brief instant, I witnessed a mixture of emotions pass across his features: sorrow, fear, doubt, resignation.

"Leave us alone!" one of the apostles growled at the group of armed men. "We've done nothing! What do you want with us?"

By way of an answer, a guard shoved the apostle standing closest to him. Then everything went crazy — men running, shouts, scuffles, torches arcing through the night sky, sketching fire trails in the air like sparklers on the Fourth of July.

The bush we were hiding behind rustled as a couple of people ran past. "Hurry," one apostle yelled. "This way!"

"Halt!" shouted a guard pursuing them.

Another commotion erupted on the other side of us. I peeked through the branches to see Peter grappling with one of the men who had accompanied Judas. A short sword scraped against its scabbard as Peter drew it out. The moonlight bounced off the blade just before the sword sliced through the ear of his opponent. A pain-filled cry ripped the night.

"Malchus!" A guard with a torch bent over the injured man who rocked back and forth on the ground with his hand pressed to the side of his head.

The apostles evaporated into the surrounding blackness, abandoning Jesus. Judas disappeared, too.

Jesus knelt on the ground in front of the injured Malchus and touched the bloody mess that a moment before had been an ear. Malchus' moaning stopped. The guards stared with disbelief. There was no more blood or pain. The ear was healed — whole once again.

The calm of shocked silence lasted but a moment, and then the guards sprung into action. In an instant, the men had Jesus on his feet, his wrists held in vise-like grips by a man on either side of him.

Again, I started to stand up. "Stay here!" Mark ordered, wedging me to the earth with a firm hand pushing against my shoulder. "Let me handle this." He started to creep around to the front of the bush.

"No!" I said through clenched teeth. I had to go. That was what I was here for, wasn't it: to stop this right here, right now? Surely, I could convince those men. After all, they'd just witnessed a miracle! Crouching behind the bush, gathering my courage to leave the security of its shadow, I made up my mind to march up to the guards and beg for Jesus' life.

I hiked my skirt up to rise when I saw a man turn away from the group. His head pivoted as he scanned the shrubbery around the perimeter. Then the torch passed in front of his face — a face turned my way.

Arrow Brows' face, his eyes flaming with anger.

CHAPTER FOURTEEN

Mark hovered on the other side of the bush, his head swiveling once between me and the guard. I hesitated, too. There was blood caked around the eczema patches on my hands. Since I didn't have my cloak to hide beneath, Arrow Brows was sure to recognize me and my "leprosy." Mark must have sensed my thought, and after a quick glance down at the cloak he was wearing — my cloak, which was now of no help in hiding me — he turned to face the man striding toward him.

"You there!" Arrow Brows yelled at Mark, but Mark didn't answer. He sprinted away from the bush — straight at the guard. Like a tight end running for the end zone, he rushed at Arrow Brows and barreled into him with a forearm shiver that sent the torch from his hand flaming to the ground.

"Stop! Stop!" the man shouted. Mark's ploy worked. Arrow Brows snatched up the torch and tore after him. Mark stutter-stepped around a large rock and hurdled a fallen tree. I could tell that Mark was letting Arrow Brows stay close in order to pull him as far away from me as possible. Maybe too close.

With a burst of energy I didn't think Arrow Brows could possibly muster, he narrowed the gap between himself and Mark in a half-dozen strides. Mark darted to the left, just as the guard reached out to snag him. Mark arched his back, but a hand of filthy fingers closed around a fold of the cloak.

Mark didn't lose a step; he merely dropped his arms to his sides allowing the cloak to slip off his body and puddle to the ground, where it tripped up Arrow Brows. The moonlight bounced off Mark's bare backside just before he cut into a darkened thicket and out of my view. Arrow Brows regained his balance, sped after Mark, and vanished into the darkness. I remained cringing behind the bush, and I turned my attention to Jesus and his captors.

They were tying him up. Jesus stood stock-still as the guards wrenched his hands together and bound his wrists and arms tightly with thick rope, apparently enjoying their job. They turned him around and shoved him in the direction they wanted him to walk, right toward where I was hiding.

The procession was a study in contradiction. The cluster of men dressed in dark robes for their sinister mission ringed Jesus in his cream-colored tunic and cloak. Their eyes gleamed with evil and hatred, but Jesus' face shone with holy composure. My fear kept me crouched behind the bush. What could I do now that would change anything?

The group passed just feet from where I cowered. As the soldiers led Jesus stumbling away with his hands bound behind his back, he turned his head slightly in my direction. Those eyes, those warm, beautiful eyes fringed with thick, black lashes and illuminated by torchlight drilled into mine, and he lowered his eyelids slowly and brought them back up: a silent acknowledgment of my presence. I didn't think anyone could see me, but he knew I was there. He had known all along.

The group passed by me, and I gathered what little courage I had left. "Wait!" I called, my voice cracking. I stepped from behind the bush. The men pivoted as one, clubs raised and swords drawn. A sword came within a hand's breadth of my face. I opened my mouth to scream, but before the cry had left my lips, somehow Jesus disentangled himself from the guards. He was standing in front of me, shielding me with his body even though his hands were still tied.

"Since I am the one you want," he said, "let these others go."

Two guards, still staggering from the shock of having their captive seemingly melt out of their hands, lunged for Jesus' arms in a panic.

"It's just a girl," one of them said, throwing a glance at me, and the others lowered their weapons.

I stepped forward, sucked in deep breaths and tried to reign in my runaway heart. My eyes darted from one guard's face to another. "You can't turn him over," I pleaded. "He's done nothing wrong. He is good and holy. Can't you see that? You are taking him to his death!"

Jesus moved closer to me, his eyes showing his complete understanding of the situation and . . . acceptance. I threw my arms around his waist and clung to him. His tunic was still damp from his profuse sweating, but he was warm and comforting. With my ear pressed against his chest, I could hear his heart beating. My body shook with sobs.

"Shhhh," he whispered, his head bent to mine, his lips brushing my forehead.

"No! No! You can't go with them. Tell them," I begged him, holding on as tightly as I could. "Tell them who you are." My voice croaked with despair. "I know you can get away! You don't need to do this. Please, don't leave us. Don't leave *me*!"

He spoke tenderly, but with firm conviction. "I tell you the truth. It is better for you that I go. For if I do not go, the Advocate will not come to you. But if I go, I will send him to you."

"No! There must be some other way. There *must* be! God can do anything!" My legs buckled and I fell to my knees, wrapped my arms around his calves, and buried my face against his knees, nearly hysterical.

"Get her out of here!" Someone shouted. "We have to move!" The guards' fingers dug into my biceps as they hauled me roughly to my feet. As if in slow motion, I saw one of them lift his hand to strike my face.

Jesus couldn't stop them with his arms, but he could with his eyes, which suddenly blazed like a lion's. The men dropped my arms.

He turned to me, and his expression softened, his eyes reflecting love and pain. Not his own. Mine. "You are in anguish," he said. "But I will see you again, and your heart will rejoice, and no one will take your joy away from you."

"I said *move!*" The guard's voice was tinged with panic now. He wheeled Jesus around and heaved him, tripping, away from me. My gut felt as if a boxer had delivered a roundhouse punch.

"No!" I screamed, but I was blocked as they surrounded him in their rush from the garden. I sank to the ground and lay there on my side, bawling like a baby, my cheek pressed into twigs and pine needles, my knees pulled up to my chest, too numb to think or act or pray.

∞

I don't know how long I stayed there. It seemed like forever. I stopped crying but started to shake uncontrollably — not only from the shock of what had just happened, but also because of the chill that had crept in and gripped the hill.

When the men were far off, I got up trembling. To give me time to think, I searched for my cloak and found it, white against the dark ground where Mark had dropped it.

A gust shook the trees, scattering shadows across the ground. The thought of finding my way back to the city by myself sent a shiver racing down my back. I took one step and stopped. What was that? Something rustled the shrubs not far from me. I stood perfectly still, willing my ears to pick up even the tiniest sound. I hiccupped back a sob, and held my breath. There it was again.

"Mark?" I called. Complete silence. Please let it be Mark coming back to get me, I prayed. Nothing. It must have been my imagination. The next instant, the underbrush exploded in a fury, and a deer rifled out, not two feet in front of me.

I fell back on my rear, my heart thundering in my ears once again. I sat for many minutes, panting as if I'd just finished a playoff soccer game. Then I rolled on my knees and stood up to find myself face-to-face with Arrow Brows.

I screamed and turned to run as Arrow Brows reached for me. His fingernails raked my shoulder, but my legs started pumping, and I raced off, tripping over stones and skirting trees. My breath rattled in my chest, and behind me, I heard a shout. Were the trees yelling at me? No. Arrow Brows was hollering for me to stop. I didn't, but pressed on, stubbing my toes and wishing I was wearing my soccer cleats rather than sandals.

Something solid hit me squarely in the back, and I crashed to the ground. He was on me immediately, smelling of sweat and wine. Grabbing my shoulder, he flipped me over so hard I thought my ribs must have broken. Spit collected in the corners of his mouth, and his eyes were hard and unblinking.

"Unclean!" I shouted, praying that the trick would work. "I'm unclean!"

Arrow Brows didn't buy it. "You don't have leprosy," he said.

"But the Pharisee said —"

"That old man is a fool," he said as he pinned me tighter to the ground and pulled out a length of the same kind of rope the soldiers had just used on Jesus.

I tried to squirm away from him. "Then what do you want with me?" It wasn't a question I really wanted him to answer.

"Not you," he said. "The other one."

I drew my breath in sharply. He had seen Mark wearing my cloak. What was the punishment for breaking that law? "Look, what happened back there with Mark —"

He snorted. "Not him. The girl!" Oh, no! My mind jumped back to yesterday. He meant Tabby.

He nearly pulled my arm from its socket as he yanked me to my feet, twisted me around, and pinned my hands behind me. He looped the rope around my wrists.

"Who is she?" he snarled. "A Gentile inside the Temple is forbidden. Tell me who she is!"

"No!" I threw myself forward in a futile attempt to get away, but I was trapped.

He laughed as he pulled the rope taut and knotted it. "Then you will answer to the priests."

"Let me go!" I screamed, adding backward kicks to my attempt to get away.

"Seraphina!"

Mark! In the light of the bright, full moon, I could see him standing several yards away, clad once again in his own damp clothes. "Let her go," he demanded.

Arrow Brows grunted and gripped me even tighter. "Go home, boy," he said.

Mark straightened his back a bit. "I'm not leaving without my sister."

We were at a standoff. In despair, I looked down at the ground. A nice oval-shaped rock, about the size of a golf ball rested in front of me. I had an idea. I eased my toe under the rock, and with a quick glance at Mark, I flicked it up to him. It was heavier than a soccer ball, and it didn't get the lift I wanted. But almost as though he knew what I had in mind, Mark stooped and caught it.

I ducked, and Mark hurled the stone like a 90-mile-per-hour fastball. I heard it thud into Arrow Brows, and he fell to the ground, dragging me down on top of him.

I rolled away from him. Arrow Brows didn't move. He must have turned his head when Mark threw the stone, because it caught him on the temple, where blood now ran from a deep cut. Mark pulled me up and enveloped me in his arms, pressing me against his wet clothes.

"Are you all right?" he asked. "Let me get you loose."

In a moment he had pulled the knots apart, and I was free of the rope. "Thanks." I looked at Arrow Brows lying on the ground. "Is he . . . dead?"

Mark knelt over Arrow Brows and felt for a pulse. "No. Just knocked out. Help me tie him up." Together, we dragged him into a sitting position against a tree and used the rope to tie his hands behind the trunk.

"He's not going to be happy when he wakes up," I said as Mark ripped a strip from the bottom of Arrow Brow's tunic and gagged him with it. Blood ran from the deep cut just above his temple.

"Tear off two more strips of fabric," I said. He did, and I wadded one up and pressed it against Arrow Brows' cut. I took the other strip and looped it around his head so that it held the makeshift bandage in place. I tied it tightly.

"Yes, you would make a fine physician," Mark said. "But he doesn't deserve it."

"Let's just make sure he can't get loose soon," I said.

Mark gave the knotted rope around Arrow Brows' wrists an extra yank. "Let's go."

We didn't talk until we reached the bottom of the hill and started to cross the valley. "Back there in the garden . . . how did you know what would happen?" Mark asked.

I stopped walking, and he turned to face me. His hair had dried into wild curls, and a smudge of dirt streaked across one cheek. His eyes searched my face in anticipation.

"You know how I knew," I said.

His eyes were dark orbs under his brow. He swallowed hard, his Adam's apple working the saliva down his throat. Yes, he knew.

"So what do we do now?" he asked.

CHAPTER FIFTEEN

"We need help," I said as we made our way back across the creek.

"Simon Peter!" Mark said. "We have to find him. He'll help."

I resisted the urge to scoff out loud. "I don't think so." Mark looked at me with a wrinkled brow.

I glanced at him as we continued to walk. "While I was gone from the upper room, Yeshua told Peter he would deny him, didn't he?"

Mark's mouth opened and closed, opened and closed as if he thought of something to say, rejected it, and came up with something else, which he also rejected.

" 'Before the cock crows twice, you will deny me three times': that's what he said, wasn't it?" I asked.

Mark nodded.

"I don't think he's going to be of much use," I said.

"Can't we convince him to help?" he asked.

"I don't know," I said. "I haven't been able to change anything so far. But I guess we could try."

"But where?" he asked. "Who knows where he is?"

"I do. The high priest's house." Mark's eyes rounded at the news.

"They've taken Jesus there. Peter will be in the courtyard. Can we get in?" I asked.

"I don't know," he said. "There's only one way to find out."

He took my hand in his, gave it a firm squeeze, and hurriedly led the way back toward the city. We came up out of the Kidron Valley and entered through a gate along the southern edge of the city. A wide set of stone stairs stepped their way up the hill and flanked a large home brightly illuminated with lamps at virtually every window.

So this was where the high priest lived.

∞

We stood a distance away from the entrance to Caiaphas' courtyard. A young woman served as the gatekeeper, admitting those she knew, rejecting those she did not. A handful of guards approached the gate, and the one in the lead appeared to be on good terms with the maid. With a brilliant smile, she swung the gate open, and the men filed in one by one. The guard in the lead joked with the young woman, and I could hear her laughing. Her attention was diverted from the gate as he showed her something he carried in a leather sack.

From deep in the shadows of a large pine tree, Peter emerged. He glanced to his right and to his left, then casually took his place at the end of the line of men and marched behind them into the courtyard, unnoticed, as if he were one of them. The gate clicked shut behind him. "So how do *we* get in?" I whispered to Mark.

He led me down a walkway circling the edge of the walled-in courtyard. A large tree grew next to the wall, its lowest branch hanging over it and into the garden. "Can you climb it?" he asked me.

I hiked up my skirt as I had done in Hezekiah's tunnel, tucking the back of it into the front of my belt, and Mark pretended not to notice my exposed legs.

"I can climb it, but I can't reach the first branch," I said.

"Here." He cupped his hands to make a step for me. "All right, up you go!" He boosted me so that my arms encircled the bough. I scrabbled up, swung my right leg over, and pulled myself along on top of the branch. I shimmied over to the wall and let myself down silently on top of it. Mark was already halfway across the limb.

I peered into the courtyard. If I was going to drop down from eight feet up, I didn't want to land in some prickly bush. The spot below looked as if it was just dirt, soft enough for a good landing. With no intention of jumping from that height, I rolled over onto my stomach, let my legs dangle into the courtyard, then inched down until my fingertips lost their grip on the wall, and I fell the last couple of feet and landed with a thud on my backside.

Mark merely leapt, cat-like, from the top of the wall and landed next to me in a crouching position. "Well done, *sivnapi*," he said, his tone tinged with sarcasm, but I had the feeling he was nonetheless impressed that I'd made it over.

"Oh, so I'm 'mustard seed' again?" I untucked my skirt and brushed dirt from my bottom. "Not 'foolish little girl'?"

He hitched up a shoulder. "Well, you *are* a girl. And little. Like a mustard seed." He placed his hand on the top of my head. "But foolish? . . . After what I have seen tonight, I think it would be better to say 'smart.' But *recklessly* smart."

I adjusted my cloak and surveyed the courtyard. It was a large rectangular area, but our tree was tucked into a dimly lit angle of the wall. No one could possibly have seen us. Some distance from us, a number of people milled around — servants, guards, and regular folks. That would make it easy to blend in.

As I knew he would be, Peter stood near a large fire burning in the center of the quad. A broad set of stairs led from the courtyard to the home's enormous portico, brightly lit and framed with pillars. The members of the Sanhedrin were assembled on the covered porch — there must have been seventy men there: priests, scribes, and elders from the community. They had gathered in what appeared to be a makeshift courtroom setting, and, among the men, I spotted Joseph of Arimathea. Jesus stood off to the side by himself, his hands still tied tightly behind his back, his head lowered, not moving, not speaking. A man was seated in front of the council, clearly in charge. He had to be Caiaphas.

Taking Mark by the sleeve, I towed him over to the fire, where he proceeded to flap his clothes away from his body, trying to dry them. Across from us, Peter stared into the blaze, the flames casting their orange glow onto his face. Every once in a while, he stole a look up at the proceedings on the portico.

I followed his gaze to the gathering on the porch. Although I couldn't make out specific words, the men's voices were loud and agitated. Some Pharisees gestured wildly at Jesus, their remarks directed to Caiaphas, who paced back and forth, a hard look frozen on his face. Jesus lifted his head and said something to Caiaphas, but I couldn't hear his words. Caiaphas let out a yell and grabbed a wad of his tunic in either hand. With another shout, he tore his garment open from neck to navel. Agitation stirred up the members of the council, and Joseph attempted to calm them, but they angrily waved him away.

The men surrounding Jesus yelled and spit at him, and some of them shoved and slapped him. I looked to Peter, who had turned away from the scene with a mask of agony covering his face.

One of the servant girls stopped next to him, balancing a large jug on her hip. He glanced up at her, and she inclined her head in the direction of the portico. "You, too, were with the Nazarene Yeshua," she said, examining Peter's face.

He feigned ignorance. "I do not know what you are talking about." He hurried away from the fire to a dark corner of the yard. Mark and I followed to find him sitting on a stone bench, staring at the ground.

"Why did you deny him?" I asked. "He needs you now. He needs you to stand up for him. They are going to kill him." Peter's head popped up, and the look of fright in his eyes faded somewhat when he realized he knew us. He waved us away, but Mark got in his face.

"You'd better listen to her. She knows what she's talking about. Yeshua has no one to depend on but his apostles."

"And you are one of them," I added.

A small group had gathered around us. Peter noted their presence, jumped to his feet in defiance, and said loudly to me, "My friend, I am not." He stomped away, but a man pursued him.

"Surely you are one of them; for you, too, are a Galilean," he said.

Peter spun on the man, cursing. "I do not know this man about whom you are talking," he shouted. The rooster's shrill cry ripped through the air — once, twice — mocking, accusing, condemning. Peter's face turned ashen. From up on the portico, Jesus lifted his head and looked in our direction, his eyes meeting Peter's and boring into them.

Peter whirled away, sobs racking his whole body. Large hands, weathered by years on the sea, cradled his head as he wept.

There was nothing we could do or say that would comfort him. He cried as if a knife had been shoved into his chest. And he was the one who had done the stabbing.

His sobs began to attract the attention of some of the guards warming themselves by the fire. They started to approach him, but Peter rushed past them and ran through the courtyard and out the gate. We quickly moved into the shadows and huddled against the wall until the guards moved along.

Mark's shoulders slumped in defeat, and tears stung my eyes. "Now what do we do?" he asked.

I swung my head back and forth. "Nothing. Unless you think you can break Yeshua out." We looked up to the portico, where guards were kicking and punching Jesus as they dragged him through heavy, intricately carved double doors, which banged shut behind them. I knew it would be no use to try to follow them. We had failed miserably.

"I better get you home," Mark said.

∞

Before he left me at my home, Mark lit an oil lamp and set it on the table next to my bed. After he had gone, I pulled the lamp closer. It looked as if it could have belonged to Aladdin, and I wondered, if I rubbed it, would a genie pop out and grant me my wish? I wasn't doing a very good job of accomplishing what I was trying to do on my own.

Mom hadn't returned, and I thought she must still be in the upper room visiting with her friends, unaware of what had happened in the last few hours. I sat on the edge of the bed, picking at the dried scales on the back of my hands and flicking the dead skin onto the dirt floor. Why was I here? God sent me here for a reason, didn't he? But if not to stop the crucifixion, then what?

I crawled under the blanket, but I couldn't fall asleep. The image kept appearing before my eyes of Jesus, wrists bound, utterly silent, being hit and spit upon. My heart raced, and anxiety gushed through my veins. I felt all jittery on the inside, as if I'd had way too much caffeine. When and how the tossing and turning ceased, I can't say, but the next thing I knew, my mother was shaking me awake.

"Seraphina! Seraphina!" Terror filled her voice. I sat up immediately, blinking in the lamp light.

"What is it?"

She sat on the bed next to me, the flame from the wick flickering across her face and casting deep shadows into the furrows on her forehead and the creases at the corners of her eyes.

"He's been arrested!" So she had heard about what had happened.

"I know," I said. "They're holding him at Caiaphas' house."

"That's right. How did you know that?" she asked.

"I was there in Gethsemane when Judas betrayed him, and he was arrested and taken to Caiaphas."

Mom tilted her head and squinted at me. "Betrayal? Gethsemane? Who are you talking about?"

"Yeshua. Who are *you* talking about?"

"Mark."

CHAPTER SIXTEEN

I shot out of bed. I couldn't have heard her right. Mark! The room seemed to tilt off its axis.

"No, it can't be!" I said. This was completely my fault. I had begged Mark to help me, and now he'd been arrested. I had to make this right. Somehow.

I grabbed my sandals, but my hands were shaking so hard, I fumbled with the straps. Finally, they were secure, and I wrapped my veil around my head.

"What happened to Mark?" I asked my mother.

"I don't know," she answered. "His mother just sent word. And what do you mean about Yeshua?"

I filled her in as quickly as possible, and her level of panic matched mine. "Yeshua arrested? I have to go to Miriam," she said.

"And I need to get Mark released." She looked at me with worry.

"I'll ask Joseph to help," I continued. She handed me my cloak and wrapped herself in one as well.

We bolted through the empty lanes, and I struggled to keep from hyperventilating. The sun hadn't even thought about rising when my mother and I reached Joseph of Arimathea's house. I pounded insistently, not caring if I woke the whole neighborhood. A sleepy servant opened the door warily, and behind him, I could see Joseph, his silver hair wild with that just-woken-up look. He rubbed his eyes and squinted at us. My mother explained the situation briefly and, leaving me with him, she hurriedly left to seek out Miriam.

"We must get Mark released. Will you take me to Caiaphas' house?" I asked.

He had the servant pour me a cup of milk. "Of course. Let me dress." I had no appetite and no interest in downing warm goat's milk, but I had a feeling it would be a long day. I held my nose and chugged it.

Clothed in his Pharisaic garb, and with his hair smoothed, Joseph grabbed a basket and filled it with a crockery bottle of wine plugged with a cork, some dates, a handful of olives, a wedge of cheese, and a couple of rounds of flat bread. He threw a cloth over the food, and handed the basket to me. "Both of them will be hungry," he said. I didn't need to ask who he meant by "both of them."

We rushed down the deserted streets, and within minutes we had reached Caiaphas' palatial home. There was no one guarding the gate, and we slipped into the courtyard where I — and Joseph, too, actually — had been just a few hours earlier. We hurried up the steps to the portico and through to the massive double doors. Joseph beat on the wooden surface. No answer. He banged even harder.

After a few moments, a servant pulled open the door, a large jug of oil in one arm and a lamp he had been filling resting on the floor next to his feet.

"I need to see your master. Now." Joseph brushed passed the man, and I followed.

"But, sir, he is not here."

Joseph turned back to the man, his robes swirling out around him. "What do you mean, not here? It is barely daybreak."

"He has gone to the Antonia. He had the guards take the prisoner to Pontius Pilate."

Joseph and I exchanged horrified looks. "Which prisoner?" he asked.

The servant licked his lips and gulped, but said nothing.

"Which prisoner?" Joseph demanded.

"The one they called 'the King of the Jews.' "

Joseph drew me to the side, out of earshot of the servant. "I must go to him. I can see my pleadings here last night did no good. I'm afraid we won't be able to get Mark released. At least, not this morning." He fished a silver coin from his pocket and pressed it into my hand. "Give this to the servant after he has let you visit Mark. I'll come back here shortly with Caiaphas — after I've seen to Yeshua. Pilate and I are on good terms. I'm sure he will listen to me." He smiled weakly and departed. I doubted he would get back here soon — or at all today.

The servant stood watching, and I eyed him warily. I would have to be the one to get Mark out of there. I looked at the coin in my hand, and a plan began to form in my mind. I stalked up to him, held the basket up, and flipped back the cloth for him to inspect the contents. "Provisions for the young man being held here."

The man eyed the wine and reached for the basket. "I'll take it to him," he said.

I snapped it back out of his reach. "No. I'm sorry, but my master has instructed me to see to the prisoner personally." I could pass for a servant girl, couldn't I? I drew myself up to my full five feet, trying to look confident and strong. Under my shift, my knees knocked together like a couple of castanets. But my bold pretense worked. He exhaled with disgust, lifted the oil flagon to his shoulder and led the way through the sleeping household to the back of the residence.

We stopped outside an ornate room adorned with brocade drapes and paneled in ebony wood. Gold-capped scrolls lined shelf after shelf — the whole Bible, I assumed, at least everything that had been written up to that time, and other texts as well. A partially unwound scroll lay on a large table that had been waxed to a mirrored sheen.

"Wait here," the servant instructed. "I need to get the key." He popped into a room across the hall, and I eyed the scrolls room. *What passage had Caiaphas sought out?* I wondered as I looked at the scroll on the table. Curiosity proved a strong draw, and I tiptoed into the room.

A polished brass pointer resting on the open parchment directed me to the exact text, and my eyes scanned the lines of Hebrew, moving from right to left.

You will see the Son of Man seated at the right hand of the Power and coming with the clouds of heaven.

The prophet Daniel. I tried to remember the passion narrative from the Gospels. This must have been what Jesus quoted to Caiaphas last night. That's what had made the high priest so mad that he tore his clothes open. If only Caiaphas had believed it.

I slipped out of the room a second before the servant emerged from across the hall, the oil jug supported on his shoulder with one hand, a key in the other.

At the end of the hall, the servant placed the jug of oil on the floor and unlocked a door leading to a winding set of stairs curving downward. No one else was around, and that fit perfectly with my plan. He left the key in the hole, and I followed him into a cold, musty cellar that made me sneeze. The whole place was carved out of the rock foundation on which the house sat. Minimally lit by a single lamp, the corners of the hallway collected shadows along with swirls of dirt and spider webs. I didn't like being down there. I particularly didn't like being there alone with him.

Like in an old wild-west movie, the key to the cell hung from a metal peg driven into the rock. As soon as the servant had unlocked the door and swung it open, a shaft of light spilled into the room, and I could see Mark sitting against the far wall, his knees drawn up to his chest for warmth. He was wearing a dark-brown tunic and cloak, his body a grim shadow against the wheat-colored chiseled rock wall at his back.

There was no way this servant was going to let Mark go; he didn't have the authority. And I couldn't expect an angel to show up to spring him, like what happened (what *would* happen in the future, I reminded myself) to Peter in jail. Or an earthquake to shake the building, opening locked doors, like what happened (again, *would* happen) to Paul in prison at Philippi. I was going to have to do this myself, so I put my plan into action. It wasn't a pretty plan, but if it worked . . .

"Thank you," I said to the servant, stretching my lips into a forced smile. I displayed my palm in which the coin gleamed from the sweat I'd imparted to it. He reached for the silver piece, and I extended my hand as if to give it to him but dropped the coin on the floor instead.

"Oh, I'm so sorry," I said as he bent to retrieve it. He had barely reached down when I drew the wine bottle from the basket and smashed it against the back of his head. He moaned and slumped to the dirt floor, covered in wine and reeking of the alcohol. Was that a sin — to hit him? I hoped not. Still, I whispered a quick, "Forgive me."

Mark was immediately at my side, his mouth and eyes wide open. "You really are a mustard seed," he said. "Small, but capable of big things."

The servant was stirring slightly.

"Drag him inside," I ordered, and when Mark did, we locked him in the cell. I snatched the coin from the dusty floor and tossed it to Mark to pocket along with the key. Abandoning the basket, we hurried up the stairs, Mark leading the way.

He paused at the top, listening, but the house beyond remained completely silent, so he motioned for me to follow, and I stepped into the hallway behind him. Muffled sounds rose up from below. The servant was regaining consciousness.

"Wait a minute," I said, spotting the full jug of oil. I positioned it on the second step from the top and tipped it over. The oil glugged out and ran down the steps in a thick coat, turning the staircase into a giant Slip 'N Slide. It wasn't much, but it would slow the progress of anyone trying to get up or down those stairs. I quietly closed the door, shielding the mess from view. I turned the key in the lock and passed it to Mark to keep with the other one.

We sneaked out the back of the house and crossed a small garden to the wall. Mark boosted me up, then easily pulled himself onto the ledge, and we both dropped down into the lane below.

"What happened to you?" I asked when we were far from the house. "You didn't think I was serious about breaking Yeshua out of jail, did you?"

"I knew you weren't," he said. "But that didn't mean it wasn't a good idea."

I cast him a sidelong glance. "Obviously, it *wasn't* a good idea."

"You could have told me I was going to get arrested."

I pulled him to a stop. "Look, Mark, I know *some* stuff that's going to happen. Not everything. I'm not God."

He shrugged, conceding the point. "Anyway, after I left you, I went home and changed clothes and came right back here. By then the Sanhedrin members had gone. I sneaked through the house and got to the top of the stairs. I was listening at the door when a guard found me. They threw me into the cell with Yeshua."

"How did you think you were going to get him out of there?"

"I don't know." He looked at me. "Maybe knock someone in the head with a full bottle of wine?"

"And Yeshua?" I asked. "How was he?"

Mark shook his head. "Not in good shape. They beat him up pretty bad."

"Did he speak to you?"

I could see Mark's thoughts gathering inside of him as if being soaked up by a sponge in the center of his body. "A little." Mark said nothing more, and I understood that whatever had passed between them was too new, too personal for him to want to share at that moment.

∞

The roads weren't crowded until we approached the northern quadrant of the city. We couldn't even reach the Antonia Fortress because so many people clogged the lane we needed to cross. Mark and I struggled to push through them.

"Did you see him?" a woman asked her companion. "He's nearly dead already."

I reached out to her before the crowd swept her away from me. "Are you speaking of Yeshua?"

She dipped her head in affirmation, her eyes filling with tears. "They scourged him and sentenced him to death. He has already taken up the cross. I saw him, on the way — he fell right here in front of me."

She stepped back and motioned to the ground. A smear of blood stained the stones at her feet. I fell to my knees and touched the stickiness with my fingers. I pressed them to my lips. Mark and I looked at each other, a single thought bouncing between us: we were too late. The hourglass had been flipped over, and the sands of time were quickly running out.

CHAPTER SEVENTEEN

"Where is he? Which way?" Mark asked the woman. She brushed her eyes with her right hand and swung her other arm to the left in a feeble attempt to point out the direction.

"We'll never get through this crowd," Mark said to me. "Let's circle around."

We rushed from the people packing the narrow passageway and sprinted westward along another road, parallel to the way in which Jesus was obviously moving. When we squeezed in with those lining the lane, their heads were craned to the right, their bodies stretching toward the approach of the condemned.

Across the way and down about thirty yards, I spotted Jesus' mother flanked by Mary Magdalen and John. Their faces, already wracked with pain, suddenly twisted in horror, and I knew they had caught a glimpse of Jesus.

I could see him then, too, his garment plastered to his bloody flesh, the weight of the cross pressing his shoulders toward the earth. His mother broke free, and a soldier made a half-hearted attempt to restrain her until he stepped back, allowing her to fall on her knees at her son's side.

The expression on her face mirrored what I had seen in a newspaper photo of a mother at her soldier son's funeral, her face contorted in grief, tears streaming down her cheeks, folded flag clasped to her breast. It was a pain so deep, I had to turn away.

How can a mother be so close to her son who is walking toward death and be powerless to do anything to prevent it? She, the one who had brought him into the world, could do nothing to keep him from leaving it. She wouldn't be able to stop his death, I knew. Could I? *Should* I?

As I looked back, the soldier shoved Jesus, and he stumbled forward, away from his mother. Mary Magdalen and John lifted Miriam to her feet, and the procession advanced toward us.

Jesus staggered on, one feeble step following another. A heavyset Roman soldier on a horse at the head of the line doubled back and dismounted, a coiled whip in his hand.

"You!" he gestured with his whip into the crowd on the opposite side of the street. "You, there. Help him carry that cross." The throng pulled back from a man with dark-brown skin and a sand-colored caftan, and I blinked. The man was Mr. Simon, our neighbor in my "other" life — the one who had been helping Mark with his car. Was that just two days ago? Two little boys in matching caftans clung to his hands, their dark eyes wide with fear.

Mr. Simon shook his head in protest. "Sir," he said, addressing the Roman soldier, "I am taking my sons home. We have just come in from the countryside."

"I don't care. Take up that cross."

"Pick someone else," Mr. Simon said, and I drew in my breath at the sight of the soldier narrowing his eyes.

"You have been chosen," the soldier replied, a smirk creasing his face.

Mr. Simon squared his shoulders, his eyes hard with defiance as he stared at the Roman. But then he turned his head slightly as if seeing Jesus for the first time. His eyes traveled from Christ's bleeding toes to his thorn-crowned scalp, then settled back down on his face. Mr. Simon's lips parted slightly, his features softened, and his head bowed almost imperceptibly.

He dropped his sons' hands as he took a step toward the cross, and both boys burst into tears. He turned to comfort them, but the soldier uncoiled the whip and snapped it in his direction.

Mark left my side, muscled his way through the people in front of us, and crossed the street. The soldier raised the whip at him, but Mark ignored him. I hurried to join him. He knelt in front of the boys and gathered them into his arms. "Alexander, Rufus," he said to them, "it will be all right." The boys whimpered against his shoulders, their eyes on their father. Mark lifted them up, one on each hip. "I'll take them home," he said to Simon, and the crowd parted to let him pass. He looked briefly at me, and then the three of them disappeared from my view.

Simon relieved Jesus of his burden and hoisted the crossbeam across his broad shoulders. With his arms raised, his sleeves slipped toward his shoulders, and I could see his biceps and forearm muscles bulging and quivering with the struggle of the weight of the wood. As Simon labored forward with the cross, Jesus stood in place, swaying slightly.

I pushed my way past a couple of people and walked straight toward him. A soldier tried to grab my arm, but I snatched it from his grip, and he let me pass. As I reached him, Jesus turned to face me.

I gasped. The crown he wore wasn't made of thorns like those that grew on my mother's rosebushes. These were spikes, needle-sharp at the tip and thick at the base. Some of them were at least two inches long. One thorn had jabbed into the skin of his forehead, about an inch above his eyebrow. I could see its outline under the thin skin, a sickly blue streak of bruising. The tip threatened to poke through his upper eyelid, which it had snared like a fish hook in a trout's mouth.

Blood trickled down his face in a dozen rivulets, and one eye was swollen almost shut. Sweat completely soaked his skin and dripped from the ends of his hair, which seemed even blacker in its wetness.

A ruckus from up ahead made me pull my eyes from his bruised face. People argued with the soldiers, and the crowd near us swarmed upon them to get in on the action. Jesus and I stood virtually ignored.

All around us, narrow passages snaked between buildings, and everyone's attention was diverted to what was going on up the road. Escape! We had but a moment to pull it off. I remembered what he had said to me in the garden the night before, but the desire to save him from crucifixion was too great.

"Come with me," I urged, drawing his hands toward me. "You can get away." He resisted my tugging.

"Please, come now!" I pulled again, and in his weakened state, he stumbled after me. I dragged him into the shadow-blackened opening of a deserted lane. This was going to work! I supported him with one arm as we staggered away.

If we could pass another two doorways, there was a staircase I could see that must lead to a lane higher up the hill. If I could get him there, if we could find a cart, or a horse, or even somewhere to hide — I lurched forward because Jesus stopped moving.

"We're almost there!" I said, pulling. He looked at me, his dark brown eyes full of love, and shook his head ever so slightly.

"You can't let them take your life!"

He gave the slightest of smiles, sad but full of gratitude.

"No one takes it from me," he whispered. "I lay it down of my own accord. I have authority to lay it down and authority to take it up again. This command I received from my Father." He squeezed my hands gently then let them drop. He wouldn't run. He would be obedient to the end.

He turned and walked back toward the commotion in the street. Back to his crucifixion.

I was suddenly hit with a clear revelation, and I felt utter shame at what I had been doing the last couple of days. I had been tempting Jesus to run away. I was no better than the Devil taking the Lord to the highest of heights and promising all sorts of things if Jesus would just do his will. I was like Peter, who had argued with Jesus when Jesus told him that he was going to suffer and die. "Get behind me, Satan!" he had said to Peter. He could just as easily have said the same thing to me.

I ran after him and reached his side as he emerged from the passageway and into the light. He was back to the place we had left just seconds before.

I wasn't meant to save Jesus; I knew that then. But my desire to do something for him was overwhelming. I pulled the veil from my head and held it up to him, to try to wipe his face. "I'm sorry," I whispered.

Jesus placed his hands on mine, took my veil, and pressed the cloth against his face. The plump soldier on the horse galloped toward us, and a whip snapped against the pavement at our feet. With the next strike, most of the leather striped Jesus' calf, but the tip of the whip caught the little toe on my right foot and split the skin. The soldier reeled the whip back in and shouted at Jesus, "Move along!"

Up ahead, Simon still shouldered the cross. Another guard shoved Jesus forward with one arm, and with a quick jerk, threw me to the ground with the other. I landed on a sharpened point of flagstone that dug into my hip. My leg prickled with pins and needles, and I couldn't stand. Jesus stumbled and fell, then rose to his feet, and with a hand that was surprisingly strong, pulled me up. Then he trudged on.

My veil had fallen to the ground, and holding my hand to my injured hip, I bent and picked up the cloth, shaking the dust from it.

The veil was in full view of the man on the horse. He sat staring at me, as stationary as a marble statue in a park, his face nearly as white. His expression frightened me, and I began to back up slowly. Joseph of Arimathea rushed to me from out of nowhere and placed a hand protectively on my back.

The soldier on the horse pointed at my veil. "*Vera icon,*" he said. "*Vera icon.*" He drew his breath in sharply and then spurred his horse away.

My Aramaic was excellent, my Greek passable, but I was sorely lacking in Latin. I turned to Joseph for help. "What did he say?" I asked.

"*Vera icon.*" His eyes dropped from mine to the veil, and his expression mirrored the soldier's. I turned the veil around so that I could see it. It wasn't merely smudged with sweat and blotted with blood. It bore the complete image of Jesus in full color — his hair, his skin, his features. Even his eye color was imprinted on the cloth.

"What do those words mean?" I asked.

"True image. *Vera* — 'true.' *Icon* — 'image.' From this time on, that is how you will be known."

"*Vera icon.*" I repeated. Veronica. My name. Ronni, for short.

I folded the veil and gently slipped it into the front of my shift, secure against my heart — my heart, which felt simultaneously broken and blessed. I spotted Jesus a half-block away, carrying the cross again and consoling a group of crying women that included my mother, Mark's mother, Mark's aunt, who leaned on the crutches tucked under her armpits, and Cleopas' wife, Mary. Jesus turned to look at me briefly before a soldier pushed him ahead once again.

Tears ran down my face. "But why me? Why did he give me this gift?" I blubbered as I pressed my hands against the cloth tucked next to my chest. "I did everything wrong. Everything. I even tried to get him to run away." The words to the Our Father sounded in my ears: *Lead us not into temptation, but deliver us from evil.* Evil. Was that me?

"I failed, too," Joseph said quietly. He led me, hobbling, to a stone bench against the wall, and we both sat. "I tried to change their minds, but to no use." His beard dusted his chest as he slowly swung his head back and forth in an arc. "They wouldn't listen. I have resigned my seat on the council. You asked me to help, and I failed you. I failed *him*." He shifted his eyes in the direction of Jesus.

"I just thought that if he didn't die, everything could have been different," I said. "We could have lived the new covenant with him here, leading us."

Joseph lifted his head and settled his gentle gaze on me. "New covenant? He spoke of a new covenant? When?"

"Last night. At supper. He said, 'This cup is the new covenant in my blood, which will be shed for you.' "

"Ahhh." His eyes locked in place and settled on a point somewhere beyond me, either seeing nothing or seeing everything in perfect clarity. Whether he was focused on the past or peering into the future, I couldn't tell. He certainly wasn't in the present.

"What does that mean?" I asked after a few moments.

He came back to the here and now and turned his full attention to me. His face was peaceful. Still sad, but stronger. "It means that neither of us could have stopped his death. And it means that Jeremiah's

prophecy has been fulfilled: 'Behold, the days are coming, says the Lord, when I will make a new covenant with the house of Israel . . .' "
His voice trailed off.

Joseph settled his look on me. "Do you know the terms of a covenant?" he asked.

That was like a contract, right? At his law firm, Dad had handled contracts all the time. "I know a little, I think."

He picked up my hand and held it between his soft palms, his gnarled knuckles like knots on wind-battered tree branches. "A covenant is made between two parties," he began. "And it lasts until one of the parties dies."

"Like marriage?" I asked.

He nodded. "Exactly. Covenants establish relationships. God made a covenant with our fathers. With Abraham, Isaac, and Jacob. With his people Israel. Do you remember what he told them?"

"I will be your God, and you will be my people." My answer was hardly audible.

Joseph closed his eyes and gently bobbed his head up and down. "Yes, but what have we done? For these past two thousand years, Israel has sinned against God. Bound in this covenant we could not uphold. But how could it be broken?"

I shrugged. How, indeed?

"God could kill off all of Israel," Joseph said. "And he would have every reason to do so. The covenant would then be dissolved. But to what purpose?" He grew quiet, his fingers stroking his beard. "God loved his people, but if they were all dead, with whom could he have a covenant relationship?"

"No one," I answered meekly.

He smiled the same way our religion teacher did when we were on the verge of a correct answer. "So if the covenant was to be ended, what alternative was there? *God* couldn't die. Could he?"

My jaw fell. It was suddenly so clear. Why hadn't anyone ever told me this before? God *could* die, if he chose to. And Jesus was God. My mind raced as I puzzled it out.

I lay it down of my own accord, he had said of his life. He came to die. But not just to die. He came to prepare his people, to establish his Church. And when he did die, that would put an end to the old covenant. Our sins would be wiped out. *And I have the authority to take it up again*, he had said. The resurrection. A new covenant could begin, sealed with his blood. A fresh start. An invitation to eternal life in heaven with him. For everyone. He had promised it to me for Dad and Steven. And those of us still here would be guided on earth by the Spirit whom he would send. *For if I do not go, the Advocate will not come to you. But if I go, I will send him to you*, he had told me.

"All along, I thought I was supposed to stop his death," I said. "I was wrong." Tears spilled down my cheeks. "I thought by being here, I was following where the Lord was leading me."

Joseph wiped away my tears with the pads of his thumbs, as soft as rose petals. "You were. If we follow the Lord, we may not arrive at the place *we* intended to go," he said.

I thought about my last two days here. "But we always end up at the place *he* wants us to be," I said.

He stroked the back of my head. "If we trust. If we believe."

"I believe," I whispered. "I do believe."

CHAPTER EIGHTEEN

I stood, one hand pressed to my aching hip and the other hand extended to Joseph. "The hill is steep. Will you help me climb it?" I asked him.

He rose on creaking knees and clasped my hand. "We will help each other."

We turned up the lane, the tail end of the crowd that had been trailing Jesus visible in the distance. Our arms linked, we marched along in step with the rhythmic percussion of metal striking metal from high upon the hill ahead.

"Did I not see Mark here?" Joseph asked.

"Yes," I said.

"How is it that he has been released? Caiaphas could not yet have heard his case. I was with him all this morning in the Praetorium."

I drew in a big breath. "Um, he wasn't exactly released." As we passed through the city walls and climbed the hill, I briefly told Joseph what had happened. He merely blew out his breath and continued on as if to say he could address that problem later. After.

∞

I already knew what I would see at the top of Calvary, but the scene grabbed me so graphically, I felt as if I'd been smacked in the face. Three crosses were planted in clear view of anyone hiking up the road and into the city, with Jesus prominently in the center.

For the first time, I understood why this height was called Golgotha, "the place of the skull." No vegetation grew on the hilltop. It was a gently rounded mass of smooth, bone-hard rock, the color of chalk, the shape of a skull, a physical symbol of death. The crosses were sunk into three of the many deep, narrow hollows chiseled into the stone.

Talking, crying, praying, and shouting filled my ears, the din punctuated by an occasional laugh. A mother hurried her son past the scene. "Don't look," she admonished him.

A Roman guard stepped in front of them, blocking their way. "Yes, boy, do look! Learn a lesson. This is what happens to those who cause trouble!"

The mother clenched her teeth and, dragging her son by the arm, she elbowed her way past the guard.

"Your highness!" one man mocked as he approached Jesus' cross. He faked a solemn bow, and those around him howled.

Another man joined in. "Your crown seems lopsided, my lord." More laughter.

With each hoot, each snicker, I wanted to slap my hands over my ears or sock someone in the gut. A cluster of soldiers huddled together, kneeling and sitting on the ground, gambling for Jesus' clothes. A roar went up from the group, and one of the men jumped to his feet, holding Jesus' cloak up high for all to see.

"Quintus, you have all the luck today!" another soldier yelled to the man brandishing the garment.

"More luck than him!" Quintus lifted his chin in Jesus' direction. I cringed at their cheers and jeers and finally turned away from them.

Off to the side of her son's cross, the Blessed Mother stood, supported by Mary Magdalen and John. My mother and other women knelt nearby, their eyes fixed on Jesus. I don't remember walking; it was more a sensation of being pulled toward the cross. People trickled past, some spitting at the cross, others cursing.

I heard the broken sound of Jesus' voice. "Father, forgive them," he rasped. "They know not what they do." I hoped that forgiveness extended to me, too.

A man stopped and shook his fist at Jesus. "You who would destroy the Temple and rebuild it in three days, save yourself by coming down from the cross."

The soldiers joined in, shouting, "If you are King of the Jews, save yourself!"

I looked up above Jesus' head to see a large placard nailed there. Three lines of text sprawled across the board, the same line repeated in three languages — Latin, Greek, and Hebrew. "Jesus of Nazareth, King of the Jews," it read. The Latin was on top: IESVS NAZARENVS REX IVDAEORVM. The first letter of each word provided the abbreviation that adorned every crucifix I'd ever seen: INRI.

Caiaphas was there, too, his black robes swishing as he paced back and forth with scribes, Pharisees, and elders trailing him like ducklings behind their mother. He spotted the sign on the cross, and his jaw hardened. "They should not have written, 'The King of the Jews,' but rather 'This man said, I am the King of the Jews,' " he said, his voice rising.

The Roman overseeing the crucifixion stalked up to the high priest. "What Pilate has written, he has written." His prolonged glare defied Caiaphas to challenge what the governor had commissioned. Tension bristled between them until the high priest broke eye contact.

"He saved others; he cannot save himself," one of Caiaphas' group muttered.

"So he is the King of Israel!" another shouted. "Let him come down from the cross now, and we will believe in him." A chorus of laughs rose up around him. One miracle or a million miracles — it made no difference, I knew. They would never believe.

The Jewish leaders and the Roman soldiers continued their mockery, but I blocked them out and fell to my knees at the foot of the cross. I saw Mark return, but if he knelt next to me, if Joseph spoke to me, if my mother hugged me, I couldn't say. All I knew was that Jesus hung there, and my heart was nailed to his. My eyes stayed affixed to his face, my knees squashed against the rock's surface, my palms and straightened fingers pressed together under my chin. His magnificent dark eyes seemed to look straight into mine. As far as I knew, there was no one on that hill but him . . . and me.

The tears streamed down my cheeks, and my body shook with sobs. So many times I had doubted God. I hadn't understood Jesus' teaching. And how many times had I sinned? I looked back over just the last few days. I remembered the argument with my mother; I broke the Fourth Commandment. I lied. I hurt others. And here was Jesus, dying for everyone, not just the Jews. Dying for me. "Lord, I am not worthy!" I whispered. "Forgive me."

He couldn't have possibly heard me, but it seemed as if his head nodded ever so slightly. I pressed my forehead against the upright of the cross, ashamed that I, to some degree, had caused his pain by my sins.

∞

Hours later, as the sun beat upon us from directly overhead, the cosmos shifted. Sudden blackness filled the sky, encasing the earth in darkness. Silence enfolded the hillside as the sun ducked out of sight, ashamed to show its face on the tragic happenings below.

No one said anything in the strange darkness, and although it wasn't cold, people gathered their cloaks more tightly around their bodies. Mourning doves called back and forth to each other, and a crow's caw punctuated the air with an eerie haunting. I glanced up to the sky, but no hint of the sun remained. These people had probably witnessed the kind of darkness that an eclipse could bring, but the timing of the abrupt absence of light at this exact moment held a significance no one could ignore.

I think everyone jumped when Jesus' voice broke the quiet as he cried out, "Eloi, Eloi, lema sabachthani?" *My God, my God, why have you forsaken me?*

Murmurs rippled through the crowd, followed by nervous chuckles. "He's calling upon Elijah to save him!" one man said.

"Such despair," a Roman soldier added.

"And anger at his God, who will not help him!" said another.

I whirled around to face them. "He's not mad at God! That's the first line of a psalm." *You idiots*, I wanted to add. The Romans didn't know the psalms, but every Jew did. Even the kids. They memorized the psalms, prayed them constantly. This one was Psalm Twenty-Two, but the psalms weren't numbered in these days, Mr. Josephson had told us. You knew the psalm by its first line. It was like the title. Jesus was inviting everyone to pray it. I knew it by heart because when each of us had to memorize a psalm for our midterm exam, I chose the twenty-second because twenty-two had been my brother Steven's baseball-uniform number.

"It was written by David," said a Jewish man I hadn't noticed before. "A *todah* hymn — a psalm of thanksgiving."

A laugh rumbled from the flabby belly of the Roman soldier who had whipped Jesus as I stood next to him on the way of the cross. "Yes, it certainly sounds as if he is thankful!"

"Every Jew here knows that psalm," I said. My eyes swept the crowd. The Jewish leaders who had insulted Jesus were standing quietly now. Some had their mouths open. Others were backing away from the cross, the expressions on their faces a mixture of understanding, horror, and shame.

Then I heard a voice begin whispering the next line . . . and the next. Another joined in. Soon, a few more people entered into praying the psalm.

"All who see me mock me; they curl their lips and jeer . . ."

Some of the offenders standing nearby lowered their eyes at this line.

". . . they shake their heads at me . . ."

It wasn't just a few voices now: almost everyone was praying. I turned to those standing and kneeling at the foot of the cross. They moved their mouths, uttering each verse, sobbing at the more poignant parts.

"Like water my life drains away; all my bones grow soft . . ."

"They stare at me and gloat; they divide my garments among them; for my clothing they cast lots . . ."

Quintus, the soldier who had won Jesus' cloak, looked guiltily at the garment he had bundled and placed next to his hammer and rope.

"But you, Lord, do not stay far off; my strength, come quickly to help me . . ."

The tone of their voices turned from one of despair and pleading to one of hope and worship.

"You who fear the Lord, give praise! All descendants of Jacob, give honor; show reverence, all descendants of Israel! For God has not spurned or disdained the misery of this poor wretch . . ."

They continued to pray, their voices growing louder, filled with trust. When those around me reached the conclusion of the psalm, I joined in: *"The generation to come will be told of the Lord, that they may proclaim to a people yet unborn the deliverance you have brought."*

A people yet unborn. Me. The deliverance you have brought: Jesus, by his death and resurrection.

As the psalm ended, Jesus drew in one last breath. "Father, into your hands I commend my spirit." He exhaled, and the earth shuddered. His body relaxed into a slump, his head turned gently onto his right shoulder. It wasn't a posture of defeat, but looked, rather, like one of prayer. His mouth hung open, tongue swollen, lips cracked like sun-parched soil. Silence blanketed the earth, but for only a moment, and then the wind kicked up with the whistling fury of a tornado.

An enormous gust gathered the dust and dirt at the foot of the cross and swirled them into a spiral that curled upward around Jesus. Like a cloud of incense, it engulfed his body and rose, carrying the essence of his sacrifice toward heaven.

A bomb-blast of thunder exploded as a bolt of lightning cut through the dark skies, striking so near me that electricity sizzled in my ears, and every hair on my body stood straight out. Men shouted and women screamed. The ground shook and knocked people flat on their faces.

"Take cover!" a man yelled.

"Get off the hill!" a soldier ordered, and many people staggered to their feet, attempting to do just that.

I gripped the cross with both hands as an earthquake's tremors quivered through me from my toes to the top of my head.

The rock-hard earth cracked at the base of the cross, and I wondered if it might topple over. But it remained firmly implanted in the ground, strong and upright.

The skies opened, and the clouds wrung themselves out upon the earth. I wasn't cold; I didn't even feel wet, but long, soaked clumps of hair lashed my neck and cheeks in the fierce wind. I stepped back from the cross. It was over. I lifted my face to the sky and inhaled deeply again and again. Rain smelled the same everywhere — whether it was pelting the barren stone hillsides of Jerusalem or polka-dotting the smooth sidewalks of suburban America. That mineral-scented tang. Heaven's tears.

The soldier who had overseen the crucifixion — the one whose whip had split my toe — gaped at what was happening around him. "Truly, this was the Son of God!" he said as he sank to his knees, a trancelike expression covering his face.

I turned around to see my mother among a small group gathered near Miriam. Mark was nowhere to be found.

Centurion Longinus rode his horse up the incline, the rat-a-tat of hoofbeats dueling with rumbles of thunder. When he dismounted and marched up to the cross a moment later, the soldier kneeling in front of it wouldn't, or couldn't, respond to his superior's orders.

"Get your lance," Centurion Longinus barked at him. "Look at me!" The soldier didn't, but I did. Mr. Long's eyes were so blood-red, he looked like a creature from outer space in some sci-fi movie. He blinked and struggled to open his eyelids again. Lightning streaked across the sky once more, and he clasped his hands to his face as a shield against the brightness.

As the lightning died out, Mr. Long tramped over to his horse and pulled a spear from its holder. A half-dozen purposeful strides later, he stood below Jesus' body and lifted the weapon like a javelin thrower.

"No!" I shouted. I extended my arms toward the lance, trying to stop him, but I couldn't reach it. He shoved the tip deep into Jesus' side. Off to my right, the Blessed Mother shrieked as if she, too, had been speared.

Blood and clear fluid gushed out of Jesus' side, spraying the centurion in the face and splashing my upraised arms. I heard Mr. Long scream and saw him reel backwards.

My first impulse was to pull my arms away and wipe the blood from my hands. Dirt always irritated my hands, and I thought that surely my skin would burn as it does when lemon juice touches the cracks across my knuckles or seeps into the cuts on my fingertips. But it didn't.

"My eyes!" Mr. Long screamed. The pain must have been horrid, but when he turned to face me, I could see that I was wrong. His eyeballs were as white as bleached linen, and his irises were the brightest blue I'd ever seen. They were just like Tabby's eyes. Healthy. Perfect. Healed.

Finally free of the agony, his brow relaxed, his wrinkles melted, and then he realized *how* he had been cured. He lifted his eyes to the Lord and fell to his knees, his back straight, his red cloak flapping in the breeze. He pulled the helmet from his head and let it roll away from him. Clenching his right fist, he struck his breast with it and left his arm there, crossed over his heart. It was the same motion I'd seen a million times in church, usually done by the old ladies who sat in the front pews and who still wore lace veils that looked like paper plates with designs cut into them. I always thought that their striking their chests was a rather funny gesture, but not today.

I knelt, too, clasped my hands together, and bowed my head. I circled the upright of the cross with my arms, laid my cheek against Jesus' feet, and gently kissed them.

CHAPTER NINETEEN

Mark and Joseph crested the hill together, and while Joseph hurried over to the cross, I ran to Mark. "Where have you been? Why weren't you here?" Had Mark deserted him, too?

"I went back into the city," Mark said, his chest heaving as he sucked in deep breaths. "I went back to the upper room. They're all there. Hiding. They won't come."

"Who?"

"The apostles. All but John." His voice broke. He glanced at the figures huddled at the foot of the cross. "And Judas," he added, lowering his eyes to the ground.

So Mark *had* deserted Jesus. What other reason could there be for his leaving? My expression must have given me away, because Mark shook his head. "I didn't want to leave," he said. "Joseph sent me. He went to ask Pilate for Yeshua's body, and he wanted me to get this." Mark pulled his arm out from under his cloak. Draped over his forearm was a folded length of cream-colored material.

I felt terrible for having doubted him. "He sent you to get the tablecloth?" I asked. "What for?"

Mark didn't answer. He went over to the cross where someone had leaned a ladder up against the back of it. Joseph and another man were laboring to remove Jesus' body. So much for the Pharisee's rule of not touching the dead, I thought. And Joseph, a Pharisee himself. Yes, indeed. Everything was different now.

Mark spread the cloth on the ground before helping Joseph and the other man lower the body onto it.

My mother leaned down and whispered something in Mark's ear. He looked over at me and then nodded to my mother. A moment later he was back at my side.

"Your mother will be staying with Miriam tonight," he said. My mom stood with one arm holding Jesus' mother, and the other hand grasping Mary Magdalen's. "She asked me to see you home. Does she know what happened this morning?"

He meant the jail break. I moved my head back and forth, almost imperceptibly.

"Jerusalem is in madness," he said. "The curtain in the Temple has been torn in two."

"And that's important because . . . ?"

His expression registered confusion at my question. Then his face transformed with understanding. "You never learned about the curtain . . . in your time?" The last phrase was but a whisper. So he believed what I had said, that what I knew came from more than just a vision or a dream.

I shook my head. "I've heard of the curtain. I just don't know its purpose."

He turned to face the city, and I followed his gaze to the gold-crowned Temple slick with rain. "It blocks off the Holy of Holies. The place where God meets the High Priest each year on the Day of Atonement. The curtain separates man from God."

I looked back to Jesus' body, prone on the cloth underneath the cross. "Not much need for that now, is there?"

Mark was silent for many moments, and when I turned to him, two tears had joined the raindrops cutting tracks down his dusty cheeks. "I guess not," he whispered. He used the cuff of his sleeve to wipe his face.

"Seraphina, come. The Sabbath is nearly here." I didn't want to leave. I felt numb and rooted to the spot. Mark gently turned me away and led me down the back side of the hill. The rumblings of thunder chased us down the embankment and echoed far away through the valley, carrying the news of what had happened here today throughout Judea and beyond.

I tripped down the rocky slope in a daze, not even aware that I'd been in this very place just two days earlier. Then the incline flattened out, and I realized that we had reached the rock quarry.

"Look!" Mark pointed at the hill we had descended. A jagged cleft ran all the way down the face of the slope. "The earthquake must have done that."

The crevice zigzagged its way down the hillside, and my eyes traced its path to where it ended. I drew my breath in sharply.

"What is it?" Mark asked.

I looked up, trying to see the top of the hill, but I was too close to it. I turned and ran away from the hillside, stopping every so often to see if the top was visible. Mark followed closely, and when we'd gotten far enough away, we spun around to face the mount.

Inky clouds draped the crest of the hill, but visible against that darkness were the even blacker images of a trio of crosses. The crevice that the earthquake chiseled into the ground originated just below the center cross and cut down through the hill like a lightning bolt.

"Oh, my," I whispered.

"What is it?" Mark asked again. "What do you see?"

"Look where the crack stops." The gap had chewed its way through the earth right into the rock quarry where it abruptly halted, not in the section of solid limestone, but in the area the stone masons had abandoned because the rock was too soft. The earthquake should have completely crumbled it, but it didn't.

"The stone that the builders rejected," Mark said.

"Has become the cornerstone," I said, finishing the quotation from Psalms.

∞

Our route home took us through the graveyard where the white-washed tombs glistened in the rain. I ran to where Dad and Steven were buried, and this time I flung myself across the top, and Mark knelt next to me, resting his forehead on the stone near my head.

I didn't think I could possibly have any tears left in me, but they gushed out and puddled on the slab. It was more death than I could handle.

"I miss them so much," I cried. "How could this have happened to them?"

Mark stretched his arm across my back and inched over so that his head was against mine. "Shhh." He stroked my hair as if I were a little kid. "It was an accident. The road to Jericho is so narrow." I hadn't literally been asking how they had died, but now it was all that I wanted to know.

"They . . . they didn't have to die. I wish —" I choked on my tears and couldn't finish the sentence as the bitterness backed up in my throat.

"Not many men would help someone they didn't know," Mark said, "especially a Samaritan. But your father and Steven were not like other men."

No, they weren't. Not in the time and place where I knew them. Apparently not here, either.

"They couldn't know that a cart would break loose and knock them off that cliff," he said. "That Samaritan was hurt, that's all they knew. They bandaged him and moved him off to the side of the road. They stopped to help because they had the kind of love Yeshua spoke of."

Mark's face took on a blank expression. "Love. A Samaritan!" he whispered. He blinked once and then settled his gaze on me. He nodded and smiled ever so slightly. "It makes sense now."

"What does?" I asked.

"I was there once when a lawyer asked Yeshua what he had to do to inherit eternal life," Mark said.

I remembered from the Gospel what Jesus had told him. "You shall love the Lord your God with all your heart, and with all your soul, and with all your strength, and with all your mind; and your neighbor as yourself," I said.

"Yes," Mark said. "And when the lawyer asked who his neighbor was, Yeshua answered with a parable."

My throat turned dry. "The Good Samaritan," I murmured.

Mark nodded. "A Samaritan who saved the life of a Jew, his enemy. On the road to Jericho."

"The same place where Dad and Steven stopped to save the life of a Samaritan," I said.

Mark placed his hands on my arms. "Not just *any* Samaritan, I don't think. *That* Samaritan."

"The Good Samaritan in Yeshua's parable?"

"Perhaps," Mark answered. "I can't be sure, but when Yeshua was telling this parable, he kept looking at me. Not even looking so much at the lawyer, but at *me*. I didn't know why, but now I think he was trying to tell me something."

"That Dad and Steven saved that man?"

"And then that man went on to save someone else," Mark added.

"But wasn't that parable just a made-up story?" I asked. A story that has changed lives for centuries.

Mark hunched up his shoulders and then let them drop. "Was it?"

What if it wasn't made up? What if there really *had* been a Samaritan who had stopped to help an injured Jew. And what if he had done that because someone who was supposed to be *his* enemy had once saved *him*? Someone like my dad. And Steven. A lump as solid as a walnut wedged in my throat.

We walked out of the graveyard in silence. The rain had lightened to a soft shower, and the sun, low on the horizon, peeked out from behind the clouds. After a few minutes, a rainbow creased the eastern sky in a crescent of color. I thought of the rainbow God sent Noah as a sign of his promise to never again destroy the earth by a flood. This rainbow was a promise, too, I decided — that no matter how bad the storm is we have to weather, a bright new day awaits.

∞

Mark touched the mezuzah and kissed his fingers before swinging open the door to my house.

"I'm glad to be back here," I said as I brushed past him.

"There's no place like home," he said.

I smiled slightly and shook my head, sending rain-dampened curls flying side to side.

"What?" he asked.

"Nothing. I was just going to say the same thing."

In her pen, Toto the goat bleated nonstop, desperately needing to be milked since I'd neglected the chore when I dashed out that morning. Mark set about the task while I stoked the fire in the kitchen. I guessed that Mark hadn't eaten anything since last night. And that cup of milk I had at Joseph's that morning seemed a lifetime away. In a way, it was.

I heated a pan and pulled out a few eggs, an onion, a pepper, and some cheese and proceeded to make a Denver omelet, minus the ham.

While it cooked, I went outside, drew some water from the cistern, and dumped the bucket over my feet. The cool water rinsed away most of the dirt and the dried blood on my foot that had been cut by the whip, but a bit remained on the little toe. I sat on the ground and used a wet rag to tend to it. I rubbed at the purple-colored tip. Was I going to lose the toenail? I examined it more closely, and it was then I realized that the nail wasn't dying; the purple color was the nail polish that remained when I had run out of polish remover two days ago.

Back in the kitchen, I folded and flipped the omelet, and Mark plunked the bucket of milk on the table. He crossed his arms, rested them high against the wall and pressed his face into the hollow they formed. I heard him sniffle once, twice.

"Don't be sad," I said, placing my hand on his shoulder. He turned his head to the side and opened a bloodshot eye at me.

I pulled my veil out from inside my gown and unfolded it gently. I thought the image might have faded or become smudged, but it shone with more brilliance and definition than before. Carefully holding the top corners, I turned it for Mark to see.

Mark fell on his knees in front of the cloth. "Yeshua, my Lord," he said, dropping his head. With more reverence than anyone ever gave the most precious piece of art, Mark picked up a corner of the veil and brought it to his lips.

"Oh, Seraphina —" he whispered.

"Not Seraphina," I corrected. "God has blessed me with the vera icon. I am Veronica."

He nodded. "Veronica," he said and nodded again. "Veronica." He sat at the table, his hands cradling his head.

I refolded the veil and placed it inside my shift once again. "Things will get better," I said. "Much better. And soon."

He looked up at me. "Really?" he asked. "You know that?"

I went to the fire, slid the omelet onto a plate and set it before him. "You know it, too," I said. "If you search your heart. If you remember all the things he told you."

"But he's dead. If he hadn't died, if he had had more time —"

"That's what I used to think," I said. "But I was wrong."

Mark's eyes flashed at me.

"He did what he came here to do," I finished.

"He died," Mark said. "Nothing is worth dying for!"

"You're wrong," I said, thinking of Dad and Steven. And the man in the striped tunic who had been trying to stop an uprising when Bar Abbas stabbed him. And Tabby, who had risked her life for me. "No one dies for nothing. He sacrificed himself for our sins. He put an end to the old and brought in the new." I knelt on the floor next to Mark. "None of us deserves God's love, but he gives it anyway. Jesus opened the gates of heaven for us. And he will lead the way there to everlasting life."

"But everything he taught us is gone along with him."

"No, it's not. Just wait until the first day of the week. You will be amazed. You'll see. His message will spread through the whole world."

Mark snorted. "How? How could that possibly happen — now?"

"The apostles will travel. They'll teach and preach."

The look on Mark's face was clouded with doubt. "Those cowards?" He shook his head. "John, maybe, but —"

"They will surprise you," I said. "They will surprise themselves." *And give their lives for the cause,* I wanted to add, but didn't.

"Men will write about Yeshua and his mission," I said. "The good news will be recorded for everyone. Forever." I stopped, and a gasp caught in my throat.

The fog of confusion that had surrounded me since I woke up in Jerusalem began to thin. Of course. How could I have been so stupid? I was never supposed to stop the crucifixion. I had realized that earlier in the day. But I *was* charged with a very important duty.

"Mark." I whispered his name. "Mark, *you* must write about him."

"What?"

I took Mark's hands in mine, and we stood up together.

"You have to write about this," I said, swinging my arm wide over the table. He looked at the table and the plate and back at me.

"Not about the food," I said. "About Yeshua. About everything that happened today. And before. And what is still to come."

"No," he said. "I couldn't. I told you, I am not a scholar."

"You don't need to be. You have much more than book learning could ever give you. You have experience. You traveled with him, saw his miracles. You spent his last night with him. And witnessed his death. Do you know how blessed you are? You have seen much, heard much, and you will learn much more in the years to come." My mind raced ahead to the future, *his* future. *You can interpret for Peter, write down his memories, travel with Paul,* I thought. *You can make a difference.* A smile played on my lips. *And so can I.*

I tapped him on the forehead. "You have his words in your head. Use them." I patted his chest. "And you have a love for him here. Go out to all the world, and tell the good news."

He bent and picked up his cloak. "I didn't mean right now," I said. "Where are you going?"

He pulled his cloak over his shoulders. "I can't stay. They'll be looking for me. If they're not already."

I felt lightheaded, and the room tilted slightly. "No. You can't leave. Not yet."

"I have to. I'm not safe staying in Jerusalem. I broke out of Caiaphas' jail, remember? I'll come back as soon as I can."

"I'll go with you." I went to the door and snatched my mantle from the peg.

He crossed over to me and took it from my hands. "No. I won't put you in danger, too."

"If you're in danger, then I'm in danger. *I'm* the one who knocked out that servant."

Mark placed his hands on my shoulders and squeezed. "No. They'll think I did it. If they question you, Joseph will protect you. You'll be safe."

My throat tightened to the diameter of a straw. "Where will you go?"

He drew the edges of his cloak together the way he did the first time I saw him standing there in my house. "I don't think I should tell you. If they ask you, it's better that you not know."

I straightened my back and squared my shoulders. "I wouldn't tell them where you are."

He ran his fingers along my cheek and cupped my chin. "I know you wouldn't. You are the strongest, bravest girl I know." A blush colored his cheeks. "And the prettiest mustard seed there is."

Now it was my turn to blush. My eyes stung with tears, and I blinked rapidly to try to hold everything back. Mark's eyes searched my face, and I wanted nothing more than to fall into those chocolate-colored pools and escape.

"Listen to me," he said. "If they ask you where I am, tell them your betrothed has left you, and you don't know when you will see him again. Then let loose with the tears. I think you can manage that." I proved it right then as the cascades coursed down my cheeks. "They'll leave you alone."

It took a minute before what he said registered. "My betrothed?" I hiccupped. "Don't you mean my kinsman?"

Crimson crept into every bit of his face including the tips of his ears. "I mean betrothed," he whispered. He leaned in and rested his forehead against mine and twirled a lock of my hair around his finger. "Someday. If I'm lucky." He lifted up my chin and pressed his mouth to mine, his lips firm in their commitment, gentle in their promise. Then he was gone.

CHAPTER TWENTY

It was the most pleasant awakening I had ever experienced. That drowsy, sleep-filled state ebbed away at a turtle's pace as my senses gradually engaged. I lay stock-still, eyes not yet opened, letting the world rouse itself around me. Birds chirped a cheery greeting back and forth to each other, their song underscored by the occasional yap of a dog. A warm breeze crept to me from outside, bringing with it the scent of spring in all its newness and life.

What a contrast to the death I had witnessed. My spirits wilted as remembrance of the crucifixion sneaked into my consciousness. It used to be the loss of Steven and Dad that was the first thing to tug at my memory in the morning. Is this how it would be for me from now on — Jesus' death seeping into life at the start of each new day? Then so be it. I knew the end of the story, and so, too, would the whole world — very soon.

Somewhere in the distance, church bells tolled, not mournfully, but with joyous abandon. I sucked in a deep breath and gently blew it out. Then it hit me. Church bells. Here in Jerusalem? In 33 A.D.? Slowly, I opened my eyes, not daring to hope for what my sight confirmed: I was in my old room. In America. Two thousand years in the future.

My nightstand was littered with wadded up tissues, a thermometer, the throw-up bowl (I must have been really sick!), a nearly empty glass of flat gingerale with a bendy straw sticking out of it, Mom's rosary, and the book she was reading, a pencil holding her place. My desk chair had been pulled up to the nightstand, and an afghan from the living room draped the back of it. How long had Mom sat there tending to me, watching over me, praying for me? Overnight? Days?

I sat up, expecting my head to throb or the walls to spin, but nothing happened. Mom poked her head into the room.

"Ah, you're awake. How are you doing?" she asked.

"Fine." It didn't matter what I answered, her reaction would have been the same. She sat on the edge of my bed, felt my cheeks with the back of her hand and then pressed her lips to my forehead.

"What day is it?" I asked.

"Sunday."

"What happened to me?"

"Strep. It came back. You had a bad case." She turned her face to the window. "Really bad." I could see her throat move as she swallowed.

"I feel great now," I said.

"Your fever broke last night."

"Good thing I didn't go to Tabby's cabin, huh?"

Mom smiled and nodded. "We know that in everything, God works for good," she quoted. Her favorite words of St. Paul's from his letter to the Romans. The verse that got her through the last year, she said.

"Is Tabby back yet?"

"Actually, they never got there. An avalanche closed the pass when they were just a couple of miles away. Had to turn around and come home."

"That's too bad."

Mom's smile spread across her face. "No, that was really very good. Something amazing happened. They went to Good Friday services."

I gawked. Tabby's family in church?

"My reaction was the same as yours," Mom said. "But to hear Cassidy Long tell it, a miracle happened." I drew my knees up to my chest under the blankets as a shiver skittered down my backbone. "You know how during the veneration of the cross, they lay the big wooden crucifix on the steps in front of the altar?"

"Yes, so we can kiss Jesus' feet," I said. I touched my lips, remembering doing just that.

"Cass was so moved by the Stations of the Cross that he went up to the crucifix, but instead of kissing Jesus' feet, he kissed his side." Mom stopped talking then. She turned away slightly, blinking and swallowing hard again.

I reached over and held her hand. "His eyes are better, aren't they?" I asked. She squeezed her lips together, lowered her eyelids, and nodded.

"Completely." She opened her eyes and turned her tear-dampened face toward me. "How did you know?"

What answer could I give? I didn't want to go down that road again. Even if she believed my story, I wasn't sure it was something I wanted to share with anyone — at least not right now. I hunched up my shoulders.

"You must have heard me speaking about it," she said. "Or Tabby. Do you remember her sitting here with you?"

No, I didn't remember. But it didn't surprise me.

She stood and gathered up the used tissues, which she tossed into the trash can. "How about if I bring you something to eat?"

"Okay. You haven't been to Mass yet, have you?"

"No. I wasn't sure I'd be able go at all if you weren't feeling better. I didn't want to leave you."

"Well, I *am* better. And I want to go."

She paused at my door. "Oh, Veronica, I don't think that's a good idea."

I climbed from bed and walked over to her. "I really want to go. I need to go."

She felt my forehead again — as if my temperature could possibly have changed in the last five minutes. "All right. Get dressed. I'll bring you a little something for breakfast. Mass doesn't start for over an hour."

She closed the door behind her. A bird trilled at the cracked-open window. The pigeon. I snagged a handful of sunflower seeds, but he flew off as I reached the window and pushed it open the rest of the way. I leaned out and inhaled the scent of dew on the new grass.

Snowball clumps of aromatic white flowers covered the crabapple tree in the yard, and the morning sun warmed the fragrance like a wick melting the middle of a scented candle. The pigeon sat on a branch of the tree, watching me.

I uncurled my fingers and extended my palm filled with the seeds. The bird swooped back to the ledge. With tentative steps, he drew closer and pecked once, twice, three times at the palm of my hand, tickling it.

From next door, a car engine sparked to life, and the Mustang inched its way out onto the driveway. Mark put it in park, got out of the car, and spotted me in the window. He leapt over the short hedge separating our yards and reached my window in three seconds flat. The bird took off, and I dumped the rest of the seeds on the ledge.

"You got it running!" I said, trying to be cool as I pretended not to notice that Mark looked absolutely gorgeous in a navy blue suit and red-striped tie.

"Yeah, Mr. Simon helped me put in a new carburetor. It's running like new." His eyes traveled over my face. "And it looks like you are, too."

"Good enough to go to Mass," I said.

"Let me drive you and your mom! Dad will sit up front with me, but you and our moms can sit in the back. It'll be tight, but . . . what d'ya say?"

"I'd love to," I answered. At least, I hope that's what I said. It could just as easily have come out, "I love you."

"You'll never guess who'll be there." His eyes twinkled like a kid's on Christmas morning.

"Would that be the Longs?"

"Aw, you already knew."

"My mom told me about what happened on Good Friday. I can't imagine why they went to church. Can you?"

"Well . . . yeah."

"Why?"

His shoulders humped up in an "aw, shucks" kind of way, and the right side of his mouth jerked into that crooked smile. "I asked them to come."

So it was as easy as that. "Go and make disciples," Jesus had said. That had always sounded like a really big job to me. But I guess it wasn't that hard to do after all. An invitation to come along. That's all it took.

Mom walked into the room balancing a cup and saucer in one hand and carrying a plate of toast with the other. "If you're going to Mass, you better get dressed, Missy."

"Can we ride in the Mustang with Mark?"

"I know I've only got my permit," he said, "but Dad will sit up front with me."

Mom looked from me to him and back again. "I suppose so. Now eat up."

I picked up the mug and sipped. Once again, a cup of warm milk, only this time it was intentionally warm, and I was prepared for it.

The grandfather clock in the entry hall chimed the quarter hour. "We'll leave in twenty minutes, Ronni," Mark said, and then he leaned in through the open window.

"I'm really glad you're okay," he whispered, his mouth against my ear. He kissed my cheek, grinned at me, and went back to his house.

I choked on the mouthful of milk but covered my surprise by turning it into a cough. I touched my cheek, still faintly moist from his kiss.

I looked at Mom, but she either hadn't seen and heard what had just happened, or she was pretending she hadn't.

I plopped into the desk chair and propped up my right foot on the bed while I munched down the toast.

"Is that toe still hurting you?" Mom asked.

How did she know about that? "Uh, yeah. What happened to it?"

She sat on the bed and placed my foot in her lap while she examined the toe. "I went to put a load of laundry in while you were sleeping. You got up on your own to go to the bathroom and caught your foot on the chair leg. You did quite a job on it."

145

I rubbed at the toe. "I don't remember doing that." I only remembered a whip splitting the skin.

"You were pretty out if it. Delirious at times. That was before Dr. Fritz came by."

"Dr. Fritz was here?" We probably had the only family doctor in town who would even consider making a house call, but he was semi-retired now. He'd been Mom's doctor when she was a little girl, so our family was pretty special to him.

"He gave you a shot of penicillin. That's what turned you around," she said. I rubbed my sore left hip, the one I'd fallen on when the soldier pushed me. "Yep, that's where you got it." She patted my calf and set my leg back down.

"By the way," she added. "Dr. Fritz is going with a group to volunteer at a clinic in Honduras for a month this summer. He thought that with your interest in medicine, you might like to go along and help."

I sat up straight. "Really? You'd let me go? But we couldn't afford it."

"Dr. Fritz said that he'd like to help sponsor you, but that most of the costs would be paid by the charity. Mustard Seed Medical Mission, I think it was."

Mustard Seed. A feeling of warmth flooded my chest. "Could I go?"

"Well, that depends," she said. "It would help if your Spanish were better." She tried not to smile, but her eyes gave her away. "Do you think you can bring up your grade this last quarter?"

"I think so," I said.

"I think so, too," she said with a grin. "Now get dressed." She gathered up the empty plate and cup and walked toward my bedroom door.

"Mom?"

"Mmmm?"

"Thank you. For everything."

"You're welcome."

"I love you."

She turned around, and for the first time in many months, I saw her face awash in peace. "I know. I love you, too," she said and quietly closed the door behind her.

I pulled the chair over to my desk and bent over the trash can, where I plowed through the discarded tissues until I had found all the bits of the broken trophy. I laid the pieces of the soccer girl out on my desk. When I got back from Mass, I'd get out the superglue and put her back together again.

I picked up the picture of Steven and Dad, and I traced their figures with my finger. "Happy Easter," I whispered, kissing each face. "I still miss you, but I'm very proud of you. And I'm going to make you proud of me, too."

Someday, I thought, we'll all be together again. Jesus had promised me. *He who hears my word and believes him who sent me has eternal life.* I had heard his word; I *knew* him, and I believed in him. And when my days were through tending to the least of his brethren as a doctor, I'd be ready for his call to join him . . . and Dad and Steven . . . in eternal life.

I pulled my bedroom curtain shut and slipped into my Easter dress, a buttery-yellow number with a floral print of red poppies. After fluffing out my hair, which had curled up nicely in black ringlets, I knelt down in front of my closet to dig for my shoes. I felt around blindly for the red leather slides, passing by athletic shoes, Crocs, my soccer cleats, flip-flops, and hiking boots. Finally, I pulled the red shoes out and sat down to put them on.

From that position, I spotted a folded square of white fabric wedged between the nightstand and my mattress. It was the tea towel that had become a veil that had wiped the face of the Lord. How much of that was true? How much had really happened? All of it? None of it?

I stared at it for several minutes, debating what to do. Finally, I crawled over to the bed, stood up, and straightened out my dress. With quivering hands, I fumbled with the material, trying and failing to unfold it. I sucked in a deep breath, labored to calm myself, and slowly opened it. The cloth was blank. I flipped it over. Nothing.

I sank to the bed, balling up the material in my lap. What did it mean? Had nothing happened to me? Had I not experienced what I was so sure I had experienced the last few days?

I thought about that for quite a while. What if I hadn't really been there at the crucifixion? Did it matter in the grand scheme of things? No, I decided. It didn't matter. What did matter was that I had a better understanding of who Jesus was and what he had done. And continues to do. For me. For everyone. "Blessed are those who have not seen and have believed," I said, echoing Jesus' words to Thomas.

I spread the cloth on my lap and smoothed the wrinkles, spreading my fingers and gently sliding them from the center to the edges, expecting the skin to snag the material, but getting no resistance. I stopped and took a good look at my hands.

No flaky scales. No bleeding cracks. No oozing bumps. Had the skin gotten better while I was sick? Could the penicillin shot have tamed the eczema? I brought my fingers closer to my eyes. The nails were smooth and flat, glowing with a healthy pink color. It would have taken weeks, months, to grow out my bumpy, yellowed nails.

Nails. My mind shifted to a different type of nail. Huge metal ones with square heads, hammered through a human body and into the wood of a cross. And a lance. Tabby's dad picking it up and piercing Jesus' side with it. My arms raised in protest. Blood and water spraying from the wound. My hands bathed in the fluid. Jesus curing me. Once again.

I sank to my knees, my face buried in my hands, tears gathering in the palms. "Thank you," I prayed. He had healed my hands, healed my heart.

My mother knocked at the door. "Ronni, Mark's here. I'll be waiting in the car."

I stood, wiped the tears from my face, and smoothed the skirt of my dress. In front of the mirror, I pulled a brush through my waves and touched a dab of lip gloss to my mouth. I hurried into the living room where the front door was open, revealing a rectangle of bright sunshine, in the center of which Mark stood in silhouette.

"Peanut," he said when I reached him. "You look beautiful."

He extended his hands and I placed mine into his. He drew me close to his chest and rested his chin on the top of my head. "Welcome back," he whispered.

I froze. *Welcome back*, he'd said. What did he mean? Welcome back from being so sick and out-of-it? Or welcome back from . . . there?

I drew back and looked him squarely in the eyes, but all he did was grin at me and wink. Slowly, he turned around, and linking his fingers in mine, he led the way down the porch steps and out into the brilliant light of Easter morning.

ACKNOWLEDGMENTS

First and foremost, I give thanks to God for his bountiful blessings, for the salvation brought by the Word Incarnate, and for the guidance of the Holy Spirit.

I'm indebted to my family for their ongoing love and support: my husband, Gary; my sons and daughters-in-law Brian and Sarah and Kevin and Christine; my grandson, Christopher John Paul; and my siblings and their families.

I have to thank my wonderful instructors at the Denver Catholic Biblical School and the Augustine Institute who opened up Scripture for me: Jeff Cavins, Deb Holiday, Thomas Smith, Dr. Edward Sri, David Walker, Wei-Hsien Wan, and especially Dr. Tim Gray, who wrote one paragraph in one of his books that changed my life and spurred the writing of this book.

My invaluable critique group helped shape this work in its early stages and encouraged me every step of the way: Hilari Bell, Jane Bigelow, Meridee Cecil, Anna-Maria Crum, Laura Deal, Coleen DeGroff, Wick Downing, Amy Efaw, Randy Fraser, Sean McCollum, Pam Mingle, Chris Perkins, Julie Peters, Cheryl Reifsnyder, Lisa Roberts, Shawn Shea, Bobbi Shupe, Caroline Stutson, and Denise Vega.

Exceptional teacher Marie Heule Enzaldo and her focus group of students at St. Mary's School in Littleton, Colorado, helped me see this book through their eyes: Maria Alcorn, Aimee Casias, Abigail Donovan, Jordan Green, Katya Larson, Katie Lawrence, Kim Morikawa, Olivia Newman, Liz Schmidt, and Jessie Simms.

I'm indebted to others who read and commented on early versions of the book or supported me with advice and sympathetic ears: Kathy Gill, Sally Kurtzman, Betsy and Whitney Lyle, Kathleen Pelley, Stephanie Reyes, Karen Schlipman, and Elizabeth Sri.

I thank Dr. Danelle Habhab and Deacon Alan Rastrelli, M.D. for their invaluable medical information.

I'm grateful to Curtis Martin, who was the key to unlocking the door to the right people. And I thank those people — publisher John Barger, who believed in this work, and especially Regina Doman, whose editorial talents and insights took this book to the next level.

For more information about this book, the author, and no-charge author visits (either in person or via the Internet), please visit:

www.claudiamcadam.com

Teachers, youth ministers, book-club leaders, homeschool families, and others can find chapter exams, a teacher's guide, book-club discussion notes, and additional resources at the website.

An Invitation

Reader, the book that you hold in your hands was published by Sophia Institute Press.

Sophia Institute seeks to restore man's knowledge of eternal truth, including man's knowledge of his own nature, his relation to other persons, and his relation to God.

Our press fulfills this mission by offering translations, reprints, and new publications. We offer scholarly as well as popular publications; there are works of fiction along with books that draw from all the arts and sciences of our civilization. These books afford readers a rich source of the enduring wisdom of mankind.

Sophia Institute Press is the publishing arm of the Thomas More College of Liberal Arts and Holy Spirit College. Both colleges are dedicated to providing university-level education in the Western tradition under the guiding light of Catholic teaching.

If you know a young person who might be interested in the ideas found in this book, share it. If you know a young person seeking a college that takes seriously the adventure of learning and the quest for truth, bring our institutions to his attention.

www.SophiaInstitute.com
www.ThomasMoreCollege.edu
www.HolySpiritCollege.org

SOPHIA INSTITUTE PRESS

THE PUBLISHING DIVISION OF